Lucy and the **Rocket Dog**

Lucy and the ROCKET DOG

By Will Buckingham

illustrations by Monica Arnaldo

ALFRED A. KNOPF

New York

THIS IS A BORZOI BOOK PUBLISHED BY ALFRED A. KNOPF

Visit us on the Web! randomhousekids.com

Educators and librarians, for a variety of teaching tools, visit us at RHTeachersLibrarians.com

Library of Congress Cataloging-in-Publication Data

Names: Buckingham, Will, author. | Arnaldo, Monica, illustrator.
Title: Lucy and the rocket dog / by Will Buckingham ;
illustrations by Monica Arnaldo.
Description: New York : Alfred A. Knopf, [2017] |
Summary: Budding scientist
Lucy builds a rocket ship and accidentally sends her beloved dog, Laika, into space.
Identifiers: LCCN 2016018144 (print) | LCCN 2016056702 (ebook) |
ISBN 978-0-399-55432-2 (trade) | ISBN 978-0-399-55433-9 (lib. bdg.) |
ISBN 978-0-399-55434-6 (ebook)
Subjects: | CYAC: Dogs—Fiction. | Space ships—Fiction. |
Space and time—Fiction.
Classification: LCC PZ7.B8799 Lu 2017 (print) |
LCC PZ7.B8799 (ebook) | DDC
[Fic]—dc23]

The text of this book is set in 11-point Candida.

Printed in the United States of America
August 2017
10 9 8 7 6 5 4 3 2 1

First Edition

For India and Liberty

Lucy and Laika

Lucy was outside in the backyard, hammering as hard as she could, when her mom called her in for dinner. It was six o'clock on a November evening, and the sky was already dark. While Lucy worked, her dog, Laika, sniffed around the yard in a friendly way. Overhead, tens of hundreds of thousands of stars winked and winked again.

"Lucy!" shouted Lucy's mom.

Bang, bang, bang, went Lucy. Laika went on sniffing. The stars went on winking.

"Lucy, come in *now!*"

Bang, bang, bang.

It was not clear whether Lucy had not heard or whether she was not listening. Sometimes, when you are concentrating very hard on something, you sort of half hear and half don't hear, or you hear but you don't

realize you hear; and when people later ask you, "Weren't you listening?" you don't know what to say because the answer is no and yes at the same time.

"Your dinner is getting cold!"

Bang, bang, BANG! Lucy sat back on the grass, which was a little damp and cold, and looked at her handiwork. Then she looked down at her clothes. They were covered in grease. She looked up to the sky at the half-moon and the tens of hundreds of thousands of stars; and when she saw the stars winking at her, she winked back. Just once, for all of them, because to wink at tens of hundreds of thousands of stars in turn would take a very, very long time.

Lucy heard the kitchen door close, and she felt her stomach rumble. "Laika! Here, girl!" she called.

The dog stopped her friendly sniffing and came over to sit next to Lucy. Lucy put her arm around Laika and gave her a hug. Laika was a big, untidy, huggable dog, more friendly than clever. Lucy could feel the dog's warmth against her side. Laika licked Lucy on the ear in a friendly but not very clever way.

Lucy looked up into the sky in search of shooting stars. She knew that the best way to see shooting stars was not to try very hard, not to stare into the darkness, but to relax and to let the darkness stare back at you, to let the stars all wink at you, and to hope—but not to hope too hard—that out of the corner of your eye you might see something flash across the darkness. A meteor, that was the proper term. Lucy loved that word. A piece of another world falling to Earth.

I love space, thought Lucy as she looked up into the sky, hugging Laika to her side. *I love its bigness, and I love its here, there, and everywhereness, and I love its going-on-forever-in-every-direction-ness.*

And then she thought, *One day, when I am older, I will go and explore the bigness and the here, there, and everywhereness, and the going-on-forever-in-every-direction-ness of space.* As she thought this, she looked proudly at *Prototype I*, standing gleaming in the moonlight.

Prototype I was Lucy's very own spaceship. It had taken her most of the autumn to build. And because Lucy did not have very much money, she had built it out of all kinds of things that she had found lying around. It is amazing what people will leave lying around. Tin cans and pieces of string and packing crates and rivets and bits of old engine and oxygen cylinders and pieces of rubber tubing and circuit boards and old computers and flowerpots. It had taken her months, but now it was almost finished.

It wouldn't fly, of course. She was fairly certain that it wouldn't fly. But it was only *Prototype I*. If it didn't fly, she would build *Prototype II*, then *Prototype III*, then *Prototype IV*, then *Prototype V*, all the way up to *Prototype Whatever*. Lucy liked to write down numbers in the Roman style—I, II, III, IV, V . . . whatever, instead of 1, 2, 3, 4, 5 . . . whatever—even though she said them in the normal fashion. It was a complicated way of writing numbers, and meant that the Romans never got very good at math, but Lucy liked those old-fashioned Roman numbers because they looked grand and important.

Prototype I was a bit ramshackle, but Lucy found it beautiful in the same way that she found Laika—who was also a bit ramshackle—beautiful. Its nose pointed up to the heavens, its sides were made of shiny metal, and Lucy had painted her logo on the side. The logo looked like two letter *L*s together, one for "Lucy" and one for "Laika," surrounded by planets and moons. A flight of small steps led up to the door, which Lucy had painted yellow. She had salvaged the door handle from when her mom replaced their bathroom door.

"What do you think of *Prototype I*, Laika?" Lucy asked.

"Woof! Woof!" Laika replied, and leaned a little into Lucy.

"Do you think she will fly?" For some reason, space-ships are always girls, so you call them "she." Lucy wasn't sure why they were girls, but that was the way things were.

"Woof! Woof!" said Laika.

Lucy thought that Laika probably didn't think very much about very much. She gave the dog a squeeze and looked out into the bigness and the here, there, and everywhereness of space. Then out of the corner of her eye, Lucy saw something streaking across the heavens. She turned her head, but it was already gone. A meteor, a shooting star, a piece of another world falling to Earth.

"Woof! Woof! Woof!" Laika said, and Lucy knew she had seen it, too.

Then she heard another voice. "Lucy! Your dinner is getting cold. Come in now!" It was her mom, standing in the kitchen door. Lucy glanced around. The kitchen looked warm and friendly and strangely far-off.

"Coming, Mom," Lucy called, and got to her feet. She looked down at her dog. "Come on, Laika," she said, and she turned toward the house.

Laika stood up, but she did not follow Lucy. Instead she continued her friendly sniffing around the garden. Lucy shrugged and went inside for her dinner. Laika stayed in the garden.

Prototype I stood alone in the moonlight, ramshackle but somehow magnificent. Laika went and sniffed at the spacecraft. It smelled funny. It smelled of oil and metal and hard work and hope.

The stars in the heavens went on winking. Tens of hundreds of thousands of stars, each one of them winking at Laika and at *Prototype I* and at the house where Lucy was sitting down in front of a dinner that was already cold.

Laika

Laika went over to the spaceship, wagging her tail, and then put her nose to the metal, very carefully, and sniffed at it. Everything smelled better at night, when it was dark and the smells were bigger and rounder and when there was nothing much else to think about. Most humans would not think that *Prototype I* smelled of anything at all. They might look at it and think, *My goodness, a rocket!* or they might think, *I wonder who built that,* or they might read the logo and say to themselves, "I wonder what that means. I wonder who L and L are." But they wouldn't think to do what Laika did, and put their noses to the spacecraft so that they might come to know it better. In fact, any human who did this might be considered to be a little bit strange.

Fortunately, however, Laika was not a human but a dog; and as a dog, she could sniff at *Prototype*

I without worrying about what other people—or other dogs—might think. She sniffed long and hard, and she smelled metal and grease and the grass that *Prototype I* was resting on, and the passing scent of a cat that had gone by an hour or so ago and seen *Prototype I* and marked it with its scent in the way that cats do. She smelled the distant traffic, and the smell of Lucy's dinner that was already cold, and the smell of at least three other dogs—all of whom Laika knew well—who lived nearby. She smelled vague traces of memory and wisps of hope.

Overhead, the stars winked. But they didn't smell of anything at all, and so Laika did not pay them much attention. She walked around the rocket several times. It rested on three feet, roughly riveted together, and she sniffed each of the feet in turn, because nothing smells exactly the same as everything else when you are a dog. That is one thing that is great about being a dog, something that those of us who are non-dogs will never know or understand.

Then Laika sat down in front of *Prototype I* and tried to think. But thinking wasn't something she was very good at, and so although she was trying to think really quite hard, the thoughts didn't quite come, and so she was mostly just sitting, with the occasional thought popping into her head now and then. Some of the thoughts popped into her head so briefly that she didn't even notice them. Thoughts didn't smell of much either, and so it was hard to take as much interest in them as in other, smellier things, things like trees and cats and humans and—best of all—other dogs. But she tried as hard as she could, and after a few moments, one particular thought started to take shape in her head, a thought that went something like this:

I WONDER WHAT IS INSIDE.

Of course, we can't know exactly what the thought was that Laika had, because Laika was a dog, and because we are not dogs—or I am not a dog, and if you are reading this, it is very unlikely that you are a dog either—it is hard for us to have thoughts that are dog thoughts, instead of human thoughts. But if it had been possible to read her thoughts, and to write them down on the page, then they would have looked something like this:

I WONDER WHAT IS INSIDE.

Laika sniffed carefully at the steps that led up to the yellow door. Then she put one paw on the first step and sniffed the second, and when she was sure it smelled good, she put a paw on the second step and sniffed the third. Everything seemed to be in order, so Laika put a paw on the third step and sniffed the yellow door.

The door smelled yellow.

How can a door smell yellow? Maybe you have to be a dog to know for certain, but that was how the door smelled. It smelled yellow. Laika licked it with her long, doggy tongue, and it tasted the same as it smelled: yellow.

Laika nudged at the door with her nose, and the door swung open. She climbed the steps in that clumsy way that dogs have when they are trying to go upstairs. Stairs are really designed for things that have only two legs and not four, and so it is hard to climb the stairs if you are a dog and to look graceful when you do. But Laika—big, untidy, huggable Laika—was a dog who couldn't very easily look graceful doing anything at all. So she climbed the steps in a clumsy kind of way and stepped into *Prototype I*.

The door swung closed with a *click!*

It was dark for a second, then there was a humming sound and a few small lights flickered on, but not enough to drive out the darkness. Laika looked around and sniffed the air. She had never seen or smelled the inside of *Prototype I* before, but it smelled of warmth and of Lucy, of rugs and cushions and comfiness. On the ceiling, which was not very high at all, perhaps only as high as Lucy could stand, there were some of those stars that you can stick on your bedroom ceiling and that glow in the night with a greenish kind of glow. Unlike real stars, they did not wink. They just hovered there in the darkness. Laika could just about make out in the darkness a thing a bit like a desk, and in front of the desk a row of buttons and knobs and dials, and behind the desk a comfy chair, and beside the chair a dog basket, where she recognized—by smell instead of by sight—one of her dog blankets, and also a small bed just big enough for Lucy, but unslept in, and a little cupboard in which (although Laika did not know it) there were lots of cans of peaches and beans and other things that you might need on a long space voyage, and side by side two empty dog bowls, above which were two funnels, and a bookshelf containing some good books, because you need good books for long journeys, and also a window looking out over the garden, a kind of porthole, and a big screen like a television screen, which was gray and quiet and did not look as if it was switched on.

A thought flitted through Laika's brain, and perhaps the thought was something like this:

MAYBE I SHOULD GO AND FETCH LUCY.

But when she turned around and nudged at the door, she found it was locked.

Laika whimpered. It felt funny to be locked in that strange little room on her own. She wondered if she was even *allowed* to be there. Perhaps Lucy would be angry with her for going where she shouldn't go, and doing things she shouldn't do.

She turned around three times, nose to tail, nose to tail, nose to tail. Then she whimpered again and tried to think another thought:

. . .

No thoughts came, so Laika jumped up on the chair in front of the desk and put her nose to the TV screen. She sometimes did this in the house when she wanted to get Lucy's attention. Lucy would then shout, "Laiiii-kaaaa!" and pretend to be angry, and pull Laika away from the TV, and drag the dog back to the sofa, and put her arms around Laika's neck, and they would lie together on the sofa watching TV, which was exactly the point, and exactly why Laika did it.

But this time Lucy did not shout. Laika's nose left a wet streak on the TV screen, but Lucy did not appear.

Laika felt confused. Again she tried to think some thoughts:

. . .

And again no thoughts came.

Then Laika sniffed at the buttons and the knobs.

As she was sniffing, she pressed one button a little too hard and the lights came on. The greenish stars on the ceiling disappeared. The room started to throb, very gently. The TV screen hummed a little and flickered, but without a picture.

Laika sniffed the buttons. She put up her paw and patted one of the smallest buttons.

A voice—Lucy's voice—said, "Security lock deactivated." Laika had no idea what this meant, but she recognized Lucy's voice and barked twice.

"Woof! Woof!"

There was no sign of Lucy. If Laika had been a human being, now she would have frowned; but instead she did whatever it is that dogs do instead of frowning. It was a more inside kind of frown thing than an outside kind of frown thing.

"Woof! Woof!" she said.

"Awaiting instructions," said Lucy's voice. Her voice seemed to come from all around. Laika could not see where.

So Laika put out her paw again and placed it on

the biggest button, and after a moment's indecision she pressed down on the button.

"Ten," said Lucy from out of nowhere.

"Woof!" said Laika.

"Nine," Lucy replied.

"Woof! Woof!"

"Eight."

"Woof! Woof! Woof!"

"Seven."

Laika looked around and started to tremble. This was strange. Nothing like it had ever happened to her before. "Owww!" she said.

"Six."

"Owww! Woof! Woof!" said Laika. And if you could translate this into human language, it might mean, *Lucy! Lucy! Where are you?*

"Five."

"Oooowwwww!"

"Four."

"Er-oooowww, errrr-ooooowwww!"

"Three."

Prototype I started to shake and to shudder. There was a roaring sound, and if Laika said anything at all, the roaring was so loud that it blotted out her voice.

"Two."

The roaring became louder and louder. Laika put her head down on the desk and put her paws over her nose, and hoped it was all going to stop very, very soon.

"One."

Roooaaaarrrrr! went *Prototype I.*

"Ooooowwwwww! Er-ooooowwwww!" went Laika.

And Lucy's voice—coming from nowhere in particular, or everywhere in general—shouted out, "Woo-hoo! We have liftoff!"

Then everything was lost in a roaring and thundering of sound as *Prototype I* tipped a little, shook itself, and lifted off the ground.

Vrrrrrooooooooooooooommmmmmmmmm!

Lucy

When *Prototype I* went *Vrrrrrroooooooooooooommm-
mmmmmmm!* Lucy was finishing her dinner and was
trying to explain something to her mom about space and
its here, there, and everywhereness; but Lucy's mom was
not really listening very hard because she had her own
problems and had her head underneath the sink, which
was blocked by something or other. It wasn't that Lucy's
mom wasn't interested in space. Space, she thought, was
a useful thing to have around. In fact, sometimes she com-
plained that there wasn't enough of it around and that she
could do with more. Lucy found this odd, given that space
was here, there, and everywhere. It seemed to Lucy that
space was one of those things that there was always more
of. You just had to look out of the window, or go into the
garden, or go for a walk, or look up at the sky at night

and be winked at by the stars, and wink back at them in turn. But Lucy's mom's view of space was that it was what people call a limited resource: like cookies, for example, something that there was only a certain amount of and that ran out far too soon.

"Mom," Lucy said, "when I've finished dinner, do you want to come and look at *Prototype I*?"

"Mmm-hmmm . . . ," her mom said from underneath the sink.

"She's almost finished, Mom."

"Mmm-hmmm . . ."

Lucy sighed. "Mom, do you want me to help with the sink?"

There was a pause, then a clanking from under the kitchen counter, and Lucy's mom popped her head out. Her hands were filled with bits and pieces of the underneath of the sink. Lucy's mom smiled. "I think I'm doing all right, Lucy," she said. "Just eat your dinner." Then her head disappeared back under the sink again.

That was the way it was. Problems with the sink were Lucy's mom's business. Building space rockets was Lucy's business. Lucy would have helped with the sink if she could, but Mom liked doing things on her own. And maybe after dinner Mom would come and look at the spacecraft and perhaps make a few suggestions—could it be painted a different color, was it pointy enough, wasn't the logo wonky?—but they would only be suggestions, because she wouldn't want to interfere.

"Mom," said Lucy, "do you know how far away Alpha Centauri A is?"

"*What* A?" said her mom's voice from somewhere among the pipes and plumbing.

"*Alpha Centauri* A," said Lucy.

"What's that?" her mom asked.

"It's a star, Mom," said Lucy, putting her knife and fork down. She was sure that she had told her mom this before.

The clanking under the sink stopped, and Lucy's mom reappeared again. She was holding more bits and pieces of sink. "Lucy, I'm trying to fix the sink," she said.

"If you guess how far it is, then I'll let you finish," said Lucy.

Lucy's mom sighed and put down the bits and pieces of sink. "All right, then," she said. "Maybe one hundred thousand miles?"

"Nope." Lucy grinned.

"More?" her mom asked.

"Much more," said Lucy.

"Umm . . . one hundred million miles?"

"Nope," said Lucy again.

"I give up!" Lucy's mom said.

"Three guesses!" said Lucy. "You have to have three guesses. It's the law."

"OK," said her mom. "Ten thousand million miles?"

Lucy looked very pleased with herself. "Not even close," she said.

"How much, then?" Lucy's mom asked.

"Twenty-five trillion," said Lucy. "Just a bit over."

Her mom thought for a few seconds. "What's a trillion?" she asked.

So Lucy picked up a pen and wrote the number out in full on a piece of paper. The number looked like this: 25,613,263,296,055.

"Wow!" said her mom.

"Twenty-five trillion six hundred and thirteen billion two hundred and sixty-three million two hundred and ninety-six thousand and fifty-five," said Lucy proudly.

Twenty-five trillion six hundred and thirteen billion two hundred and sixty-three million two hundred and ninety-six thousand and fifty-five is a big, big number. It doesn't seem that big when you first look at it. You can write it using only fourteen digits, and there are lots of words with that many letters. Lucy knew a few of them: "uncontrollable" (that's what some people said Laika was); "indecipherable" (that's what Lucy's teachers said her handwriting was); and her favorite, "disingenuously," which means the way you say things when the things you say aren't quite right, or when you don't quite mean them. When you think about it in that way, when you say the number is just made up of fourteen digits, then you find yourself thinking that twenty-five trillion six hundred and thirteen billion two hundred and sixty-three million two hundred and ninety-six thousand and fifty-five is not a very big number at all; but when you think about it in another way—for example, when you start thinking about walking that many miles—it is very, very big indeed. In fact, it is eye-wateringly big. It is so big that when you think about it for a little while, you have to sit down in a large, comfortable chair and try not to think about anything at all, just to recover. And Lucy's mom didn't really have time to sit in armchairs not thinking about anything at all, particularly when the sink was blocked and there was a pile of washing-up to be done.

Lucy's mom looked at the number; but Lucy could see by the expression on her face that she wasn't really thinking about it very hard. She wasn't thinking about it in the way that you have to think about these things to realize how strange and wonderful they are.

"That's a big number," said her mom.

"You're not thinking about it," said Lucy.

"I'm thinking about the sink," said her mom. Then she added, trying to take an interest, "What's the star called?"

"Alpha Centauri A," said Lucy.

"Oh," said Lucy's mom. "That's a nice name."

It was at this point that they heard the strange rumbling that was coming from the garden. Lucy's mom first thought that perhaps it was a rumbling coming from the sink, and so she popped her head back between the pipes; but the rumbling didn't seem to be coming from the pipes. It seemed to be coming from outside. She came out from under the sink again and looked at Lucy.

"Lucy," she said, "what's that?"

Lucy bit her lip. The rumbling got louder.

Lucy's mom went over to the window. She could see *Prototype I* gleaming in the moonlight. It was shaking a little and giving off steam.

"Lucy," said Lucy's mom, "it's coming from the garden."

Lucy got up and went over to the window. *Prototype I* was definitely shuddering and shaking. Then a flurry of sparks came streaming out from underneath. *What's happening?* thought Lucy. Then she thought of Laika. And just as she was having this thought, from underneath *Prototype I* there was a burst of red and gold, and a huge, great balloon of fire.

Vrrrrrroooooooooooooommmmmmmmmmm!

Lucy's mom stood with her mouth open. She wanted to say, "What's going on?" She wanted to say, "Watch out for my garden, young lady!" She wanted to say, "You mean that thing can *fly?*" She wanted to say, "How are we going to explain this to your dad?" And she wanted to say, "How on Earth . . . ?" But because she wanted to say all these things at exactly the same time, something that is impossible, she just opened her mouth and a strange sound came out, a sound that sounded like this: "Ahhh—ohhh—hurrr . . ."

"Laika!" shouted Lucy. "Where's Laika?"

Prototype I lifted itself up very gently on top of the

balloon of fire for a few seconds, then—faster than you could really see it happen—it shot upward toward the tens of hundreds of thousands of winking stars.

Lucy threw open the back door and ran into the garden. The garden smelled of burned flowers and burned grass and burned earth. But Lucy wasn't paying any attention to the garden. Instead she was looking up to the sky, where a great red-and-gold streak, with a shining silver rocket at the topmost end of it, was heading farther and farther upward. The stars continued to wink, but in a way that seemed less friendly than before. And Lucy watched as the rocket got higher and higher, until it could no longer be seen, although the red-gold streak could still be made out, tracing a line across the sky.

"Laiikaaa!" Lucy shouted. "Laaaiiiiikaaaaaa!"

But Laika was already miles and miles away, and could not hear her.

"Laiiiiikaaaaaaa! Laaaiiiiikaaaaaa!"

Lucy felt tears in her eyes. She stood in the burned garden and sobbed to think that she would never see Laika again.

Lucy's mom stood in the doorway, looking at her flowers and her garden fence and her once-beautiful lawn; then she looked at Lucy, a sad little figure in the kitchen light. She sighed and stepped into the garden; and she put her arm around her daughter.

"Don't worry," she said. "Laika will be back." She said this to make them all feel better, but she wasn't sure she believed it.

"But how . . . ?" Lucy asked, looking up at her mom.

"She'll be back," said Lucy's mom. And then she felt herself beginning to cry as well. "I'm sure of it," she sniffled.

Lucy thought she didn't sound very sure.

The two of them stood there for a long while, in the middle of the burned garden, looking up at the sky.

Laika

Laika put her paws over her eyes and whimpered as *Prototype I* lifted itself off the ground in a great plume of smoke and fire and determination, hovered for a few seconds above the garden, then shot upward into the air with a noisy *Vrrrrrooooooooooooommmmmmmmmm!*

"Owwwwwowow!" said Laika. But there was nobody to hear her. She was alone in the spacecraft, and even if Lucy had been close enough, the roaring of the engines was so loud and so terrible that it would have drowned out Laika's voice. In fact, Laika couldn't even hear *herself.* All she could hear was the vrooming of *Prototype I's* engines.

Prototype I began to accelerate, to get faster and faster; and as it accelerated, it shuddered even more.

LUCY, thought Laika.

She wanted to be with Lucy. She wanted Lucy's arms

around her neck. She wanted Lucy to tickle her tummy. She wanted to be sitting in her dog basket, thinking homey doggy thoughts.

LUCY, she thought.

Then Laika began to feel very funny indeed. She suddenly felt very heavy, as if somebody were sitting on her. She tried to lift her paws from over her eyes, but her paws were heavy, too. She tried to lift her chin from where it rested on the desk, but her chin was heavy as well. Laika, who had never experienced anything like this before in her life, started to whimper. "Errerrrr-rng . . . ," she said.

She opened her eyes to see, in front of her, the flickering of the television screen. It seemed to be experiencing some interference, so it crackled and hummed and didn't make any kinds of useful sounds at all. On the control panel beneath the television set, lights flashed on and off.

"Errerrrrrng . . . ," said Laika. "Errerrrrrng . . . errerrrrng . . . ooo owoowoo!"

The rocket was traveling even faster now. It trembled in the way that no thing on Earth should tremble. But then the rocket was no longer on Earth. In fact, with every passing second, Earth was farther and farther away. The trembling turned to shuddering, and the shuddering to shaking, and all at once there was a terribly loud *BOOOOM!* as *Prototype I* broke through the sound barrier, which meant that now it was going faster than 768 miles an hour.

It was a *BOOOOM!* loud enough to wake up people who were sleeping peacefully on Earth below. Loud enough to knock birds off the perches where they had gone to roost for the night. Loud enough to make cats, stalking around their territory, stop and sniff the air, their whiskers quivering. Loud enough for Lucy, far below, to look up to the sky and say to herself, "Well, I never, that must be *Prototype I* breaking the sound barrier," and then to think, *Poor Laika! My poor faster-than-the-speed-of-sound dog Laika! What will become of her? When will I ever see her again?*

There is no denying that the speed of sound is really very fast for a dog. But *Prototype I* did not slow down when it reached the speed of sound. Instead, it shot away from Earth at even greater and greater speeds. One thousand miles an hour . . . two thousand miles an hour . . . five thousand miles an hour . . . ten thousand miles an hour . . . twelve thousand . . . fifteen thousand . . . Soon *Prototype I* was going more than twenty-five thousand miles an hour, and still it accelerated. The TV screen continued to crackle and hum, and a prerecorded voice came over the loudspeaker system. It was Lucy's voice. "All passengers," it said, "we are pleased to announce that we have now left the earth's atmosphere. Enjoy your trip."

Laika looked out of the window. The sky was filled with winking stars. Everything was so strange and different that it was as if Laika were noticing the stars for the first time. She pressed her nose to the window to see if she could smell them.

Lucy

When Lucy's dad came home, he expected to be greeted as usual by the sound of Laika's excitable barking, but instead, as he walked up to the front door, the house seemed somehow somber and silent.

Lucy's dad had been out all day, walking in the park and thinking, because he was a philosopher, which meant that he was a person whose job was to think about stuff. He sometimes wrote books about the things he thought about, and he also sometimes taught students how *they* could think about things; but mostly he just spent his time thinking interesting thoughts. Lucy's mom, in other words, was the practical one, and her husband, Lucy's dad, was the dreamy one. They were really very different from each other. Lucy's mom often said that a philosopher was no good when the sink needed unblocking; but she had to admit that he was *very* good at thinking impractical and dreamy thoughts, and sometimes this could be useful, too. Or, even when it wasn't useful, at least it could be interesting.

That evening when Lucy's dad came to the door, the house seemed very dark and gloomy; and because it normally looked cheerful and happy, this made him a bit worried. He put his key in the lock more carefully than usual, pushed open the door, peeped in, and called out, "Hello!"

When Laika didn't come bounding out to meet him—it is strange that a man who so much liked thinking about things, and a dog who didn't do very much thinking at all, should get on so well, but that is how it was—Lucy's dad called out, "Laika! Lucy! Darling!"

The "darling" was for his wife, Lucy's mom. Lucy's mom came out of the kitchen, still covered in grease from under the sink. She looked very serious.

"What's happened?" asked Lucy's dad.

"Laika has gone," said Lucy's mom.

"Gone? Where?"

"Umm . . . ," said Lucy's mom.

"And Lucy?"

"She's upstairs."

"Oh," said Lucy's dad.

"There's another thing," said Lucy's mom. "I think you should come and see the garden."

So Lucy's mom took Lucy's dad by the hand and led him through the kitchen to the back door, and when she opened the door to the garden, Lucy's dad saw that everything was burned to a crisp.

"Hmmm," he said, because that is something that philosophers say a lot.

Then he saw that *Prototype I* was missing.

"It's gone," he said.

He thought for a bit longer. You could see his brain working as he thought about the mysterious disappearance of *Prototype I* and the equally mysterious disappearance of Laika. "Where has it gone?" he asked.

Lucy's mom pointed up toward the winking stars.

"Oh," he said. "Oh . . . wow." And although he was worried about Laika and about Lucy and about the garden, he found himself thinking that if his daughter had built a spacecraft that actually worked, then it was very likely that she was the cleverest daughter in the whole wide world. The thought made him smile, just for a moment. But then he thought again about Laika and about Lucy. "I'd better go and see Lucy," he said.

Lucy's dad went upstairs. Lucy's bedroom was dark, the door open just a crack. There, standing by the window, was Lucy. In front of her was the telescope that her mom and dad had bought her for the previous Christmas. The telescope was made of brass. It stood on a tripod and was pointed out of the open window up toward the heavens. Lucy was peering through the telescope, her eye pressed to the eyepiece. Every so often she moved the telescope, scanning the sky, little bit by little bit. When her dad came closer, he saw that there were tears streaming down his daughter's face. Lucy's dad coughed to get her attention. Lucy took her eye from the eyepiece, wiped it dry with her sleeve, sniffed, shook her head sadly at her dad, and then put her eye back to the telescope and continued searching.

"Lucy," her dad whispered.

Lucy didn't reply.

Lucy's dad went over to stand next to her. When he put his hand on her shoulder, he could feel the sadness of her.

"*Prototype I* worked," Lucy's dad said softly. He couldn't help saying this with a note of pride, even though he also felt sad at the same time.

"Laika's gone," said Lucy.

"I know," said Lucy's dad.

"Mom says she'll be back, but I . . ." Then Lucy pushed away the telescope and looked at her dad. "I don't know," she said. "I don't know if she'll ever come back. She went into *Prototype I* by mistake. . . . She must have pressed a button. . . . I didn't even think it would fly. . . . We were having dinner. . . . Laika was still outside. . . . She must be *so* lonely. . . ."

And at the thought of Laika's loneliness, Lucy began to sob.

Lucy's dad put his arms around her and gave her a hug. "I'm sorry," he said.

"Dad?" Lucy asked. "Do you think she'll come back?"

Lucy's dad looked at her. He did not know what to say. "I'll have to think about it," he said, because although he wasn't very practical, he was good at thinking about things.

"And then?" asked Lucy.

"And then," said Lucy's dad, "we'll just have to see."

So Lucy wiped her eyes and went back to the telescope and continued to look at the stars. Lucy's dad turned to go. "If you need us," he said, "we'll be downstairs."

"Thanks," Lucy whispered.

"Don't stay up too late, Lucy."

"I won't," she said.

Her dad left the room and closed the door behind him.

Lucy continued searching the sky for Laika; but it is a difficult thing to find a small, solitary floating dog among the winking stars and the here, there, and everywhereness of space. She looked and looked and looked until her eyes got tired with looking. Then she turned away from the window.

Laika

The roaring and shuddering began to subside to a quiet background hum, but Laika still felt very, very heavy, as if she were made not out of bits and pieces of dog, but instead out of bits and pieces of lead, or something else very heavy. She moved her paws from her eyes and looked around, without raising her head.

"Acceleration will continue until further notice," said Lucy's voice out of nowhere in particular. Laika's ears pricked up to hear Lucy's voice, but when she looked around, she could not see her. *STRANGE,* she thought.

Then the spaceship turned a little, and out of the window Laika could see the beautiful blue-and-green face of Earth, with its seas and its mountains and its grasslands and its cities that spread across the planet's dark side in a spiderweb of light. The planet was so strange and so beautiful that Laika, although she did not know what she was looking at, stared at it in doggy amazement.

BALL? she thought. *BALL?* Then she looked around to see if she could see Lucy, because Lucy was good at throwing balls, and Laika was good at catching them, and throwing and catching balls was so much fun for both of them that they could happily spend an entire evening doing just this and nothing else.

So Laika looked at the ball, and she thought, *BALL?* and then she barked out loud several times to see whether Lucy would appear and say to her, "Here, girl!" and pluck the blue-and-green ball from where it was hanging in the blackness of space and throw it for her to play fetch.

What Laika couldn't know was that this was not just an ordinary little ball, but instead it was an unimaginably enormous planet, one that no dog could ever get its jaws around, let alone fetch. And she couldn't know that somewhere down there, on this miraculous ball, was her old home. She couldn't know that somewhere down there was the house that she had shared with Lucy and Lucy's mom and Lucy's dad, and the garden where she used to like sniffing around, the river down by the warehouses where Lucy used to take her for walks, and all the comforting and exciting smells. And, most of all, she couldn't know—because space is hard even for humans to think about, let alone dogs—that somewhere down on that beautiful blue-and-green ball was Lucy, looking and looking and looking through her telescope, then hugging her dad and sobbing, and murmuring Laika's name over and over, afraid that she might never see her dog again.

Lucy

Lucy went to bed late. And if she didn't cry herself to sleep, it was only because she had cried as much as she could cry for one evening. She lay there in the dark, her curtains still open, the cold stars winking at her, and she thought of Laika and her farness, and how she might never see her dog again, and she felt sadder than she could ever remember feeling.

This wasn't how it was supposed to happen. It should have been Lucy and Laika together—girl and dog, dog and girl—bold adventurers voyaging to the stars, with only each other for company. Then, when their adventures were over, they would have come back to tell everybody about the wonderful things that they had seen: the planets and the nebulae and the black holes (not that you can see black holes, because they are so very black that you can only sort of see around them, rather than actually seeing the holes themselves), and white dwarfs and red dwarfs and all those other kinds of stars with strange names, and asteroids and meteoroids and comets with long tails that stretched hundreds of thousands of miles across space.

But now Lucy was stuck on Earth, and Laika was far gone, heading upward and upward into the here, there, and everywhereness of space, and *Prototype I* was gone, too, so there was no way of following her, and Lucy didn't really think she'd have much chance of her parents letting her build *Prototype II*, given what *Prototype I* had done to the garden.

Lucy lay looking at the stars for a long time, and at last she fell asleep.

That night, Lucy had sad and jumbled dreams. When she woke the following morning, the Laika-lessness of her life seemed even more sad and desolate than it had the night before. She went down to breakfast and didn't feel like toast or cereal. She just sat there at the table, swinging her legs in a kind of upset way, and her mom and dad didn't know what to do with her.

After breakfast Lucy's dad told her that he was going to the park for what he called his philosophical perambulations, which meant, more or less, that he was going to the park to walk around and to think about stuff. And because on that particular morning, there were a lot of things to think about—about where Laika was; about the here, there, and everywhereness of space; about what do to about the charred garden; about whether anything would ever grow there again; and above all about how to console his daughter, who was clearly so very sad that she didn't want toast or cereal—and because these were all such big things to think about, and because Lucy looked like she could use some company, he said, "Would you like to come with me? We could perambulate together."

Lucy smiled a sad smile. "OK, Dad," she said.

So Lucy and her dad went to the park together, and they perambulated in silence. They perambulated along the paths that led through the trees. They perambulated around the duck pond three times in the clockwise direction and three times in the counterclockwise direction. They perambulated to the playground with its swings and slides and merry-go-rounds. And eventually they perambulated their way to the park café, where for a short while they stopped their perambulations and sat down, and Lucy's dad ordered a coffee and asked Lucy what she wanted, and Lucy shrugged and ordered a cup of hot chocolate.

As they waited for their drinks to arrive, they looked across the park at the dogs and the squirrels and the trees. Normally, Lucy's dad would have thought quite hard about these things. He often thought about squirrels. He was not sure why, but he found squirrels really rather good to think about. But today he didn't feel like thinking about squirrels. He had other things to think about. He was, as they say, preoccupied.

The waiter arrived with the drinks and put them on the table. Lucy's dad took out some money and paid him. Lucy looked at her cup of hot chocolate and carefully rotated the cup on its saucer a few times, but without spilling any of the hot chocolate.

"Dad?" she said.

"Mmm?" he said.

"Dad, I miss Laika."

Her dad thought about this for quite a long while. Then he said, "I know. I do too. She was a good dog."

That is all they said, because they were having such deep and difficult thoughts that they couldn't quite find the right words to say anything more.

Lucy and her dad finished their drinks in silence. Then, hand in hand, they went home.

Laika

Laika was puzzled. She was puzzled by the fact that when she barked and barked at the ball, Lucy didn't appear. She was puzzled by the strange heaviness of her paws, her snout, her ears, her everything. And even if she didn't know that Lucy was already far away *down there,* while she was far away *up here*—because she had no idea that *down there* was in fact down there, and that *up here* was up here—and even if she didn't know that she was already thousands upon thousands of miles from home, she did know this: Things had all of a sudden become very strange. Things smelled funny. The heaviness that made her feel as if she were no longer made of bits of dog was not right. And even if Lucy's voice was here, it was weird that Lucy wasn't. Putting all these things together in her mind, Laika was anxious, her poor little doggy heart unhappy and ill at ease. She started to whimper again.

Laika whimpered for a long time. She did not know how long exactly, because dogs do not know about time in the way that their owners know about time. When dog owners meet in the street, they talk about what is going to happen next week, or what they saw on television last night, or what has changed since the last time they met, or what their opinions are on the fall of the Roman Empire, or whether they think that in the future people will have special helicopters that they can strap to their backs. And while they talk about all these things, their dogs sniff at each other, and say hello to each other, and don't really think very much at all about past and present and future.

Of course, dogs have *some* sense of time. Anybody who has owned a dog will know that a dog has very strict ideas about when it should be given its breakfast, or when it should be given its dinner; and anybody who has been about to take a dog on a walk will know that the dog understands that *any moment now* it will be going on a walk. In fact, if we were to list the kinds of things that human beings think about time, the list could include some of the following questions:

Is it time for dinner?

Are we going for a walk now?

Do you want to go to the movies tonight?

Do you remember what it was like when you were young?

Do you know what year the king of Spain set his trousers on fire?

How much time do we have left until we have to go?

What is time, anyway?

Do the future and the past exist?

Do we really have the time to ask all these stupid questions?

But if you could ask a dog to think of some questions about time, then the main questions would be things like these:

IS IT MEALTIME?

IS LUCY GOING TO GIVE ME A TREAT?

IS IT TIME TO GO FOR A WALK?

No dog has ever asked what year the king of Spain set his trousers on fire. No dog has ever sat and pondered the question of whether the future and the past exist. And perhaps that is why when you go for a walk in the park, you can sometimes look at dogs and their owners and notice that the dogs look very happy, while their owners look terribly worried: because the dog owners are worrying about yesterday and tomorrow and all the things that might happen, or that have happened, while the dogs are just sniffing around, being dogs.

So Laika, although she was already thousands of miles from home and was zooming ever farther off into space, wasn't thinking, *WHEN WILL I GET BACK TO LUCY?* or *WHAT WILL HAPPEN TOMORROW?* or *WHY DIDN'T I GO BACK INTO THE HOUSE, INSTEAD OF SNIFFING AROUND* PROTOTYPE I? It was not that she didn't care about Lucy. It was not that she was confident that tomorrow would look after itself. It was only that she was a dog, and these are not the kinds of things that dogs think about.

41

In fact, what Laika was really thinking was something like this:

ERRERRRNG . . . ERRERRRNG . . . ERRERRRNG . . .

And because she was thinking these things out loud, she made funny little noises that sounded more or less like this: "Errerrrrng . . . errerrrrng . . . errerrrrng . . ."

And all the while she was thinking *ERRERRRNG . . . ERRERRRNG . . . ERRERRRNG . . .* and was making strange little "Errerrrrng . . . errerrrrng . . . errerrrrng . . ." noises, she was hoping that the terrible things that were happening to her would stop very soon.

And whether it was soon or not, it is very hard to say; but at last the heaviness began to lift, and Laika found that she could move her legs.

"Woo-hoo!" said Lucy's voice out of nowhere. "Reaching cruising speed."

Laika looked about her. Again she couldn't see Lucy. She barked once, the friendly bark she gave when Lucy came home from school, but there was no reply.

Lights were flashing on the console in front of her. Laika started to feel lighter.

And lighter . . .

And lighter . . .

Lucy

The next evening, Lucy sat down with a pen and paper, and started to do some sums. If Lucy was a bit like her dad in the way that she liked to have big thoughts and big dreams, she was also a bit like her mom in the way that she was really very practical and sensible. So Lucy started to do sums and calculations, to try and work out where Laika and *Prototype I* may have gotten to.

It was difficult, though. It is hard to tell the trajectory of a spaceship when you have a dog at the controls, inquisitively pressing all kinds of buttons with its nose, and generally making things a bit more complicated. If Lucy had been in the rocket, she would have known how to get it back down to Earth. But even for a dog, Laika wasn't very clever, so Lucy didn't think that the chances of Laika finding her own way home were very great.

Nevertheless, Lucy did her best. She did sums and calculations, and when she got tired, she put down her pen and went to look through the telescope. *Where are you, Laika?* she thought. *How can I get you back?*

It was like looking for a needle in a haystack, she thought. Or it was like looking for a needle in a thousand thousand thousand haystacks. In the middle of the night. While wearing dark glasses.

But still, Lucy looked and looked, scanning the sky with its stars and planets and comets, hoping that she might spot *Prototype I,* with its logo that linked two letter *L*s. She looked until she could no longer keep her eyes open. Then at last she went to bed.

I'm going to keep on looking, Lucy thought as she lay in bed. Then she said out loud, "Laika, I'm going to keep on looking." It was a firm decision. And it made her feel a little better. Then she turned on her side and went to sleep.

So every night after that, when she had finished her dinner, Lucy went up to her room. She took out her notebooks and her library books and her pens and pencils and her pocket calculator. She set up her telescope. And then she set to work. Sometimes she did sums and calculations. Sometimes she read books. Sometimes she just sat and thought about things. And sometimes she looked through her telescope, even though she never saw anything other than stars and planets and the here, there, and everywhereness of space.

As time went on, a number of things started to happen. Grass eventually started to grow back in the place

where *Prototype I* had burned holes in the lawn. Everyone, more or less, got used to the fact that Laika was no longer around, although they were still very sad indeed. And Lucy's mom started to get worried by the way her daughter was spending her evenings looking through her telescope, doing calculations, and looking lost in thought. "Lucy, love," she said one evening, "you know that Laika is probably not coming back."

"I know," said Lucy. After all, Lucy was a really rather sensible kind of person. She wasn't the kind of person that you can easily fool. The kind of person that you can easily fool isn't the kind of person that can build a spacecraft in her back garden out of bits and pieces she has found lying around, and can do such a good job of building it that it blasts off into deep space, carrying a solitary dog. So Lucy knew her mom was right, that there was almost no chance of Laika returning. "I know," she said. "But I'm going to keep on looking."

Lucy's mom folded her arms. "You're not planning on building another rocket, are you?" she asked.

Lucy grinned. "Of course not," she said, because she wasn't. "Even if I did, I wouldn't know where to find Laika. There's just so much space for a dog to get lost in."

"Then why are you spending your evenings in your room? It's not good for you, you know."

Lucy thought for a while. Then she smiled. "It's OK, Mom," she said. "I'm fine. But I have to keep looking and thinking and doing my sums and calculations. I owe it to Laika."

And although Lucy's mom didn't really understand

what Lucy meant, she could see that this was important to her. "You know," Lucy's mom said, "Laika was such a good dog."

"I know," said Lucy.

"Let me know if you ever need to talk."

"Thanks, Mom," said Lucy. "I will."

Laika

How strange it all was! First, after blasting off, Laika had felt really, really heavy, much heavier than any dog on Earth, much heavier, even, than the time that she had broken into the cupboard and eaten up all the dog biscuits, and Lucy had found her lying on her back on the kitchen floor, her belly full of them. But now, instead of going back to feeling normal, she started to feel unusually light. In fact, she felt so light that she started to *float*. Her ears became like strange, floppy wings on either side of her head, undulating a little as she moved. Her paws became detached from the desk. And all at once she drifted up, so that she was suspended in the middle of the spaceship, with nothing underneath her and nothing above her, and nothing to either side other than empty space.

"Enjoy the flight!" said Lucy's voice from out of some place that was hard to pinpoint.

Laika barked again. Why could she hear Lucy's voice but not see her? What was going on?

Laika was not at all sure that she was enjoying this strange, new floaty sensation. And because she was a floppy kind of dog, with ears that flopped and a tail that flopped and fur that flopped and jowls that flopped, her floppiness became floatiness instead, so that all of a sudden she had ears that floated, and a tail that floated, and fur that started to undulate with floaty kinds of waves, and jowls that floated and wobbled to either side of her face, where before they used to hang down. Laika let out a surprised yelp and floated up to the ceiling.

She sniffed the ceiling, nudging it with her nose. The nudge, although only very gentle, sent her floating off to one side of *Prototype I*. There she put a paw to the wall and pushed, very gently, and soon she went floating back across to the other side of *Prototype I*, where her backside collided with the television screen.

Laika had a thought.

THIS IS STRANGE.

Or perhaps it wasn't a thought. Perhaps it was an unease down in her bones and her sinews and her guts. But whether it was a thought or not, there was a kind of strangeness to being Laika at that moment, floating there in *Prototype I*, and the strangeness only increased when a voice crackled out from the loudspeakers. Again, it was Lucy's voice.

"Crew alert! Crew alert! It's breakfast time, everyone!"

The word "breakfast" was one of the words that Laika recognized. Lucy had, in the past, done friendly experiments on Laika and concluded that she knew several words and phrases. Things like "No!" "Good girl!" "Breakfast!" "Walk!" and "Bad girl!"—and, of course, "Laika." Laika, in other words, knew how to understand more words in human language than most humans know how to understand in dog language.

"Breakfast" was one of the words that she knew. Whenever anybody said "breakfast," Laika had a clear and unmistakable thought.

BREAKFAST.

So Laika started to look around excitedly, because breakfast was so exciting that even floating in midair couldn't dampen her enthusiasm.

Then there was a crunching noise, and from the funnel above the dog bowl on the left came dog biscuits; but instead of rattling into the bowl as they normally would, they formed a small brown cloud, a dog-biscuit cloud, and the cloud floated and dispersed throughout *Prototype I,* so that in a few moments there were dog biscuits everywhere, floating, here and there, and Laika, who was very hungry and who was floating too, opened her mouth, trying to catch now one, now another. She managed to snap at a small cluster of dog biscuits as they floated past her nose. Another few biscuits she missed. She bobbed toward the edge of the cabin and put a gentle paw on the wall. This sent her in the other

direction, right into the middle of a dog-biscuit swarm. She opened her mouth and caught them the way big fish catch little fish while swimming in the sea. They tasted the same as normal, nonfloating dog biscuits, but it was a strange sensation just opening your mouth and letting them sail in.

Laika was starting to feel a little thirsty from all the dog biscuits when a tap popped out of a hatch above the second dog bowl and squirted out a large splash of water. But the water did not fall downward; instead it drifted like a strange kind of jellyfish, transparent and wobbly, across the spaceship. Laika managed to use her front legs to propel herself through empty space in the direction of the water. She opened her mouth, and the wobbly splotch of water floated inside. She clamped her jaws shut. It was wet just like normal water, only floatier. She swallowed hard.

The loudspeaker crackled again. "Enjoy your breakfast," said Lucy's voice as Laika opened her mouth again and chomped on another five or six biscuits.

All of this started to be quite a lot of fun, for quite a long while; but eventually Laika had eaten all the biscuits and had all she needed to drink, and there was nothing more to do but float around and wonder what to do next. So Laika floated and floated, and the lights on the control panel of *Prototype I* flickered on and off, and the images on the screen changed very slowly, and outside the window the stars winked, and there was nothing other than the hum of machinery, and Laika felt in her bones that she was more alone than she had ever been before. Laika thought she might like to have a nap, but it is strange sleeping when you are floating in the middle of empty space, and when she closed her eyes, she just bumped into things.

Laika bobbed over to the window and looked out into space.

"*Owwwwowww!*" she said.

But there was nobody to hear her.

"*Owwwowwwowww!*" she said.

The stars looked back at her blankly.

"*Owwwowwwwowwww!*"

And it was then that Laika began to tremble with a terrible trembling, because everything was so very strange and so very disorienting, and because she had no idea what was happening to her. Her legs shook, her tail shuddered, her body trembled, her eyes went a bit funny, and she lost whatever reason she had (and, as she was not the cleverest of dogs, that was not very much) and went a bit loopy. Her legs started to flail around, she made odd yelping noises, and she started to bounce around the inside of *Prototype I* in panic, crying out, "*Owwwowwwwowwww! Owwwowwwwowwww! Owwwowwwwowwww!*"

It was in the middle of all of this that Laika spotted something strange outside of the window of the spacecraft, something that looked curiously familiar. There, thousands upon thousands of miles from Earth, floating in the middle of space . . .

. . . was a bone.

Lucy

Time passed, and although Lucy didn't forget about Laika, she found that the sadness eased a little, and that looking through the telescope felt a little different from how it had felt before. In the first few days after Laika was gone, she had desperately looked for *Prototype I* among the vast darkness of space. But as days turned to weeks, and weeks to months, she found herself spending less and less time looking for the one thing that she couldn't find out there in space—her dog, Laika—and more and more time looking at all the other things that she *could* find there: the stars and planets and the rings of Jupiter, the beautiful ice-crystal tails of comets, the strange craters in the moon that people once thought made shapes like faces and leaping rabbits, but that were only craters made by meteoroids crashing into the surface of the moon and leaving holes and pockmarks. And looking through the telescope became less of a sad kind of thing, and more of the kind of thing that had about it a sort of beauty, and a kind of calm.

There are some people who look deep into the blackness of space and it makes them shudder. They think about the millions and millions of stars, and the millions and millions of planets, and the black holes that are so black that you can't see them, and the countless galaxies, and the uncountableness of the things of the universe, and—worst of all—that great, vast sea of blackness, and they shudder. They think, *How scary!* or *Oh dear! How sad that makes me feel!* or *My life seems so unimportant and miserable, because I'm so very, very small, and things are so very, very big!* and they go around in a terrible gloom that makes them unfriendly, and causes them to kick stones and tin cans in a peevish fashion, and that makes them no fun to be with. But there are other people who look deep into the blackness of space and they find that, little by little, it makes them happier. They feel really rather cheerful to think that they are a part of the here, there, and everywhereness of things, to think how it is completely, gobsmackingly amazing that they are staring up at the winking stars and that the stars that are billions upon billions of miles away are winking back at them, and knowing how funny and wonderful it is that any of this is here at all, they find themselves going around with a spring in their step, that their worries are less worrying than before, and that the irritations of their lives are less irritating; and, in short, they become really rather nice people to spend time with, the kind of people you'd like to invite for tea or you'd like to meet when walking down the street.

The more Lucy gazed into space, the more she became this second kind of person, so that the more she gazed up at the stars, the more everybody said that she was exactly like the kind of person you'd want to meet. And sometimes, because she was such an agreeable person, who talked with such enthusiasm about stars and planets and galaxies and nebulae and all those other strange and big things, people would want to talk to her. Then they would ask her, "Why do you spend so much time staring through your telescope?" In reply, she would look a little bit sad and say in a voice that was just a little bit quiet, "I do it for Laika." And they would say, "Who is Laika?" And in reply, she would tell them about how Laika had blasted off in *Prototype I*. And they would say, "But surely, she will never come back?" And Lucy would say, "Perhaps not." Then she would smile, and everybody would think, *What an agreeable person this Lucy is. She is a little odd, no doubt. Perhaps she is a little more interested by the stars and planets and the here, there, and everywhereness of space than is normal. But she is agreeable nonetheless.*

You cannot be sad forever. At least, you cannot be sad in the every-moment-hurts kind of way forever. The sadness doesn't disappear, exactly; but instead it settles down into something different, a mixture of remembering and gratitude and regret and wondering. And this is what happened with Lucy. And so some time later—not the following year, but the year after—the grass that had been burned by the fire that came from the engines of *Prototype I* had grown back, and Lucy found herself one summer night lying on her back and gazing up at the winking stars, while the scent of flowers drifted on the night air. She thought about how beautiful it all was, and thought about Laika and hoped that wherever she was, she was happy and that she had enough dog biscuits to eat. And she thought about how staring at the stars made her feel closer to Laika, and then she said to herself, out loud, "Oh, Laika! The stars and planets and the here, there, and everywhereness of space are so beautiful. I don't *ever* want to stop looking at them. And somewhere out there, perhaps you are too." Then Lucy imagined Laika, wherever she was, looking into the sky. And among the winking stars and the vastness of space, she imagined a little dot looking down on Laika. And this dot was the earth, Lucy's home. And although the distances were so unimaginably huge, this thought made Lucy feel a little bit closer to Laika.

It was around this time that Lucy started to get good marks in school science classes. They were not just slightly good, haven't-you-done-well marks, but *really* good marks. They were so good that when her science teachers saw Lucy coming into the room, they would start to sweat, just a little bit, and their lips would start to tremble, and you could almost hear them thinking, *I hope Lucy doesn't ask me any difficult questions today.*

Take, for example, Mr. Kingham. Mr. Kingham— whose first name was Wilbur, something that embarrassed him a good deal—was a nice man. He always wore those shabby brown jackets that teachers like to wear, and he had a brown briefcase and an untidy gray beard and scuffed shoes, and he smiled nervously all the time, and there was nothing at all wrong with him, except that he was not very good at science.

No, that is not fair. Mr. Kingham was *all right* at science. He was *good enough* at science. Some of his pupils did well, and some did less well. He was *not exactly bad* at science; but he was a man who never looked up to the stars and thought about the here, there, and everywhereness of space, or thought, *How beautiful it all is!* He was a man who thought that being a scientist was just a job, like being a plumber or a prime minister or a pope. He was a man who, when he went home, didn't read science books like Lucy did. Unlike Lucy, he didn't go to the library every week to read impressive magazines like *New Scientist* or *Scientific American.* Instead he read detective novels, and not even particularly good ones. So every time he saw Lucy in his class, he started to shake a little in fear, because he knew that she would ask him questions. Questions like, "What would happen if you tried to go close to the speed of light?" Or questions like, "What does the inside of a black hole look like?" Or questions like . . . well, all kinds of questions that Lucy, who spent a lot of her time reading impressive magazines and science books and looking at the stars and thinking very, very hard, wanted to know the answers to. Because the more that she knew about these questions, the closer Laika seemed to be.

Laika

A bone? In space?

Thousands upon thousands upon thousands of miles from home?

What *was* going on?

Laika's mouth started to water. She floated toward the porthole and peered out, watching the bone getting bigger and bigger and bigger. She pressed her nose to the glass and sniffed. She expected a good, meaty smell. But once again all she could smell was window.

THIS IS STRANGE, Laika thought, not for the first time.

Her mouth felt funny. Her eyes were telling her mouth that this was a bone, and so it should start watering. But Laika's nose disagreed and told her mouth that it was nothing of the sort, so it should stop watering.

Confused by the mixed messages that her mouth was getting from her nose and her eyes, Laika didn't know what to do.

As her nose, her eyes, and her mouth did their best to resolve their differences, Laika floated and bobbed in front of the porthole. It was all very perplexing.

On the one hand, being a dog, Laika was inclined to trust her nose more than her eyes.

On the other hand, the bone was getting bigger and bigger and bigger. Laika's tongue lolled. She swallowed hard.

Then the bone got so large that it filled the porthole with its gleaming whiteness; and Laika's eyes told her nose to shut up, because her nose clearly didn't know what it was talking about.

BONE, Laika thought.

BIG BONE!

BIG, BIG BONE!

Lucy

"Relativity," said Lucy to Mr. Kingham, her hand up. Her eyes were eager, and she was almost bouncing on her seat in her enthusiasm.

Mr. Kingham sighed. "Lucy," he said, "I really think that this is a bit difficult for the class."

"Not at all," Lucy said. "The theory of relativity is relatively easy." She grinned at the joke, even though she knew it wasn't a very good one.

Mr. Kingham looked at her and blinked in a despairing kind of way. Lucy would be leaving this summer for another school. And Mr. Kingham was proud in a way because she was his best-ever student. Nevertheless, he would be glad to see the back of her, because she asked all kinds of awkward questions, and that made him uncomfortable. He was the kind of teacher who thought that teachers should know all the answers and their pupils should know very little, and all the teachers then had to do was to pour answers into the heads of their pupils the way that you pour tea from a teapot into a row of cups. Except when you pour tea out of a teapot, the teapot ends up empty, but when you pour answers into somebody else's head, they stay in your head as well.

But the point is this: that Lucy always had lots of questions. And Mr. Kingham didn't know how to answer these questions. This perplexed him a great deal.

"Relativity," Lucy said.

"I know what you said," Mr. Kingham replied. "But relativity is not relatively easy. It is relatively hard."

The joke was even less funny the second time around, when Mr. Kingham repeated it. Lucy just frowned. "It is easy," she said. "You just have to think about it in the right way."

Lucy loved the theory of relativity. It was a theory that had been proposed by a man called Einstein, who lived a long time ago. Einstein was a scientist who liked pulling funny faces. Lucy admired this about him. Not enough theories were invented by people who liked pulling funny faces. Or, perhaps, not enough of the very clever people who came up with new theories dared to be photographed pulling funny faces in the way that Einstein did. And if you haven't heard of this theory of relativity, it is perhaps because you are surrounded by people like Mr. Kingham, who think that things like the theory of relativity are very, very hard, and so they never bother to tell you about them. Which is a shame because, as Lucy said, it's not very hard at all.

Lucy had taught herself about the theory of relativity by reading magazines like *New Scientist* and *Scientific American* because Mr. Kingham didn't really understand it very well. And because it was her favorite theory, she wanted to explain it to the rest of the class. Lucy was the kind of girl who had favorite theories in the same way that her classmates had favorite music or favorite TV shows.

"Let me show you," Lucy said to Mr. Kingham; and before he knew it, she had jumped up from her seat and was standing by the blackboard (Mr. Kingham was old-fashioned, so he insisted on using a blackboard, with proper chalk and everything).

Lucy drew a diagram of what looked like the earth; and on the earth she drew a stick person, a stick person that looked a little bit like her. Then she drew a diagram of what looked like a rocket, and put an arrow pointing to the rocket. Underneath, at the other end of the arrow that pointed to the rocket, she wrote the words "VERY FAST." And then next to the rocket she drew something else, something that looked very like a bendy clock.

"It's a bendy clock," said one of her classmates, a boy called Owen, who was the kind of boy who knew a bendy clock when he saw one.

"Why have you drawn a bendy clock, Lucy?" asked Mr. Kingham. When he asked the question, he sounded sort of sad and a little weary.

"Because," said Lucy, "when you go very fast, like

in a rocket or something, time goes all stretchy and squishy. That is what the theory of relativity says."

"Rubbish," said Owen.

"Oh dear," said Mr. Kingham.

"It's not rubbish. It's been proved," said Lucy. "Hasn't it, Mr. Kingham?"

"Lucy, this is a bit difficult for the class," said Mr. Kingham.

"No it's not. It's easy," said Lucy. "What it means is that if I put Owen in a rocket . . ." Here she drew a picture of Owen's face looking out of the porthole of the rocket, and the whole class laughed. Owen glowered. "If I put Owen in a rocket and made him go very, very fast, and if we just stayed here, then if he went fast enough, let's say at six hundred and sixty-nine million nine hundred and forty-six thousand miles an hour, which is ninety-nine point nine percent of the speed of light . . ."

"Lucy . . . ," said Mr. Kingham, scribbling down the figures, "please."

But Lucy just went on anyway. ". . . and if Owen went that fast for, oh, I don't know, let's say one month, then by the time he got back, he would have spent only one month traveling in the spaceship, while for the rest of us . . ."

Mr. Kingham was beginning to perspire rather heavily. Lucy paused because here she had to think a bit. She screwed up her eyes and did the sums, which were not the easiest sums in the world.

"For us," said Lucy, "almost *two years* would have passed."

"Two years? That's weird," said Owen.

The rest of the students were sitting with their mouths open. They had never heard anything so strange and unlikely in all their lives.

"It's to do with the speed of light," Lucy said. "However fast you are going, the speed of light has to be the same. It's the law. So although Owen is going really fast relative to us, the speed of light has to be the same for all of us. Which means, when you work it all out, that everything else—time and space and things like that—gets super squished. Don't you see?"

The rest of the students continued to sit with their mouths open, which suggested that they didn't see at all. Then Mr. Kingham interjected. "Did you do the sums in your head, Lucy?" he asked, his eyes wide in awe and wonder.

"Yes. It's easy to work out. Let me write the equation on the board. . . ." And she started to write out the equation, which looked something like this:

$$t = \frac{t'}{\sqrt{1 - \frac{v^2}{c^2}}}$$

"Isn't that right, Mr. Kingham?" asked Lucy.

Mr. Kingham frowned, as if he was thinking very, very hard.

"The equation is indeed correct, Lucy," he sighed, after a long pause. "But I suppose we should check the sum." He got out his pocket calculator and tapped away for quite a long time. Eventually he looked up. "Two years," he said, "minus five or six weeks." His voice was slightly weak and wobbly.

Lucy shrugged. "Yeah," she said nonchalantly. "I didn't bother mentioning the five or six weeks. . . ."

Mr. Kingham stared at her. Lucy had done the sum *in her head*. He found this terrifying.

Then Mr. Kingham coughed. "OK, Lucy," he said. "Your sum is perfectly correct. But I think that you will find this is *my* classroom. Could you please sit down?"

"OK," said Lucy, perfectly pleasantly, because she really hadn't meant to be any trouble. And she went to sit down.

Mr. Kingham wiped the sweat from his forehead. He sat for a few seconds with his head in his hands, wondering what to do with his clever pupil. He liked to think of time and space as nice tidy things. Time was a thing that could be split into little boxes, like a school timetable. And space was much the same. You only had to look at Mr. Kingham's desk, the way he kept everything in what he thought was exactly the right place—the pencils lined up with the pens, the tidy stack of notebooks, everything at right angles, everything just so—to know what Mr. Kingham thought about space. And although he had learned about relativity when he was younger, he tried not to think about it too much, because it seemed a terribly *untidy* kind of idea, even if it was right. And when it came to ideas, Mr. Kingham was more interested in them being tidy than he was interested in them being right. But when he looked up, he saw a whole classroom full of hands in the air. Everybody except Lucy, who was smiling happily, and Owen, who was frowning and was clearly still thinking about what would happen if he were put in a rocket and sent far away from the classroom.

"Yes, Laura," Mr. Kingham said, pointing to a small, unhappy-looking girl with her hand up.

Laura, her eyes huge, said, "So if Lucy is correct, and if that sum is correct, then if Owen went even faster in his rocket, by the time he came back home, we'd all be very, very old?"

Lucy grinned. "Yes," she said. "If Owen went really, *really* fast, by the time he came back, we'd be super-old, like we were his grandparents."

"That's weird," said Owen for a second time.

But then the bell rang for the end of the class, and everybody—Owen and Lucy and Laura—left the classroom, leaving only Mr. Kingham behind, who sat at his desk and stared out of the window, as if he had been hit by a comet, or an asteroid, or a meteorite.

Laika

Laika gazed out of the porthole. The bone came closer and closer, and got bigger and bigger.

BIG, BIG BONE, thought Laika.

This was as big a thought as she could muster. If she had been a much cleverer dog—if she had been more clever than any dog has ever been—she might have wondered how it could be that a bone could be that big; because if it was really a big bone, then the animal it came from must have been even bigger. Bigger than any animal that had ever lived. Bigger than an elephant, or the biggest dinosaur you could ever imagine, or a blue whale.

A second time Laika had the same thought. *BIG, BIG BONE.* A bit of drool came out of the corner of her mouth and started to drift—a floating ribbon of drool—across the inside of *Prototype I.*

Outside the window the bone started to turn around in the middle of endless, dark space, so that after a few moments it was facing *Prototype I*.

The bone hung there for a little while, in the middle of space. And Laika hung there for a little while, looking out of the window, in the middle of *Prototype I*, thinking the thought *BIG, BIG BONE* and drooling. Laika's nose kept trying to tell her mouth that it clearly wasn't a bone, because it didn't smell like one. But Laika's mouth had made up its mind, and eventually Laika's nose gave up and went into a sulk.

Then something happened that, as far as we know, has never happened before in the history of the world.

The bone swallowed the dog.

Lucy

Relativity was a strange business, Lucy thought. From one point of view, if you could do the sums, it was relatively easy. But from another point of view, it made your head spin until you were dizzy. It tangled you up in all kinds of odd speculations. It made the world a little bit puzzling. And this wasn't a bad thing, because puzzling over the world was something that could be quite a lot of fun. Because Lucy was exactly the kind of person who liked puzzling over things, she decided that when she eventually finished high school, she would go to university to study astrophysics.

Although a long time had passed since they were both in Mr. Kingham's science class, Lucy was still friends with Owen. Owen still wasn't very good at science. But Owen was perfectly happy with this state of affairs. And although he didn't like sums and things like that, and he wasn't very practical and couldn't mend sinks and things, he was very good at drawing, so he decided to become an artist.

One day Lucy called Owen on the telephone. "Owen," she said. "I'm going to study astrophysics! I want to be an astronomer."

Owen was really excited by the news. "Astronomy? Oh, brilliant!" he said. "I'm a Pisces!"

"You're a what?" asked Lucy.

"My star sign," Owen said. "I'm a Pisces. Aren't you a Capricorn?"

Lucy sighed. "Not astrology, Owen. Astronomy."

"Same difference," said Owen, because it was all the same to him.

"No it's not," said Lucy sternly (Lucy could sometimes be stern if she needed). "Astronomy is a proper science. It's about planets and stars and the here, there, and everywhereness of space."

"What's astrology, then?" Owen asked her.

"Astrology is about star signs, and telling the future, and working out whether you are going to be lucky in love. It's not real science. It's just stuff that people make up."

Owen paused for a few moments. "Oh," he said thoughtfully. "Well . . . you *would* say that. You're just a typical Capricorn."

Lucy sighed. Sometimes it was so hard to get people to understand what you were talking about.

• • •

The following year Lucy started her studies. She moved into a small, cozy room at the university, and the first thing she did was to put up a big poster of Einstein pulling a funny face. She then unpacked her telescope and stood it by the window so that in the evenings she could look at the sky.

Lucy started her classes. Her professor was called Professor Cassiopeia. She was tall and serious-looking, and she always wore smart jackets. Some people were a little bit scared of Professor Cassiopeia because she looked as if she was terribly, terribly clever, but in fact she was one of the nicest people around, the kind of person you could ask to look after your cat while you were on holiday.

At the end of Lucy's first year at university, Professor Cassiopeia took Lucy's class on a trip to the Observatory on the Hill. The observatory was a place that you went to observe things—not ordinary things, but big and exciting things like stars and galaxies and nebulae and planets and moons. The observatory was in the middle of the desert, a long way from any large towns or cities, and through the roof of the observatory poked a giant telescope that pointed up to the heavens. If you want to look at the stars and to see them properly, it helps to be somewhere very, very dark. You can't see many stars in the city because there is too much other light; but if you go to a place where there are no streetlights, you can see thousands upon thousands of them.

They were a small group: Lucy, seven or eight of her friends, and Professor Cassiopeia. They left early in the morning. They had to catch a bus, then a plane, and then another bus to get out to the observatory. They arrived in the late afternoon, tired out. But when they got to the Observatory on the Hill, they forgot all about their tiredness. The sun was setting, and they could see the satellite dishes and telescopes and domes of the observatory, and they all felt a thrill of excitement.

The observatory, Lucy thought, looked a bit like a medieval castle. But it was better than a castle, because castles are built by people who think that the world is big and terrifying and has to be kept away, while observatories are built by people who think that the world is amazing and exciting, and who want to find out as much about it as they possibly can.

The director of the observatory gave them a guided tour. They saw the computers and all the complicated equipment and the telescopes and even the observatory kitchen, where the astronomers went to chat and to make coffee, and where they often had their best ideas.

The director, a severe-looking man with a fine mustache, was an enthusiastic guide. The tour took two hours and ended at ten o'clock at night (astronomers are a bit like owls, and they prefer the night). But when the director waved goodbye, and the little group headed back down the steps to the parking lot to return to the bus, Professor Cassiopeia noticed that one seat was empty.

"Hmmm," said Professor Cassiopeia. "Has anyone seen Lucy?"

"No," everybody chorused.

Professor Cassiopeia sighed. She got off the bus and strode back up the steps of the observatory. She knocked on the door. The director popped his head out. "I think we've lost one," she said.

. . .

It took a little while to track Lucy down, but at last Professor Cassiopeia and the director found her in the room with the biggest telescope of all. She was sitting peering into the eyepiece of the telescope, and when they came into the room, she did not look around.

Professor Cassiopeia thought that there was something about the way Lucy's shoulders were hunched that made her seem a little sad. "Lucy," she said softly, "we need to go."

Lucy did not move. Professor Cassiopeia glanced sideways at the director. Then she went to stand beside Lucy. She cleared her throat. "Lucy," she said again, "come on."

Then Lucy took her eye away from the telescope and looked at Professor Cassiopeia and the director, and they saw that she was crying. "Lucy, what's wrong?" they asked.

Lucy shook her head. "Laika," she said. "I'm looking for Laika."

The director and Professor Cassiopeia didn't really know what she was talking about, but they smiled the kind of smile that means, *Oh, well, I'm sure things will get better.* Then Lucy wiped her eyes and smiled bravely back.

"Come on, Lucy," Professor Cassiopeia said, "the bus is waiting."

"OK," said Lucy.

The director watched them both as they headed down the steps together. *What a strange evening,* he thought. *I wonder what was wrong with that poor girl. And I wonder who Laika is. . . .*

Laika

The bone swallowed the dog. There is no other way of saying it. The big bone, gleaming whitely, bigger than any bone that had ever existed on Earth, turned in space, and one end opened up like a giant door, and it zoomed toward *Prototype I,* with Laika still inside, and swallowed the spaceship whole.

Bump. Bump. Thud. Crunch.

Laika yelped as *Prototype I* thudded to a halt inside the bone. Then Laika, who after a few days of floating in space was getting used to the sensation of her ears flapping lazily by her sides, found herself coming down to ground with a bump.

Now, if you were somebody like Owen, and didn't really understand these things, you might ask, "A few days? How is this possible? Haven't years and years passed since Laika's liftoff?" But fortunately you are not somebody like Owen, and so you already know that relativity makes the passage of time a bit bendy and strange, and you already know that because Laika was going so very fast, and Lucy wasn't, then what was several years for Lucy was only a few days for Laika. And if you were somebody like Lucy—and not many of us are—you would be able to do the sums, and by thinking about how much time had passed on Earth, and how much time had passed in *Prototype I,* you would be able to work out exactly how fast the spacecraft was going. And you would be even more amazed at Lucy's skill, because *Prototype I* would be faster than any spacecraft had ever gone before.

As *Prototype I* bumped and crunched to a halt, a small shower of dog biscuits, and other bits and pieces that we needn't think too hard about, came raining down around Laika. She put her paws over her eyes. Outside there was the sound of a hiss. Then the door of *Prototype I*—which had traveled so very far and so very fast, but which was after all only *Prototype I,* not *II,* or *III,* or *IV,* and so was in need of some refinement—fell off with a clang.

Laika lifted a paw from her eyes. She struggled to her feet. Her tail quivering, she trotted out of *Prototype I* and down the steps.

Laika emerged into a huge, open room with walls made of gleaming metal and enormous pipes and lots of things that flashed and beeped and hummed. It must have been six times as long as Lucy's garden, and three times as wide, and as tall as a five-story house. *Prototype I,* from the outside, looked very small, and very battered. It looked like a spaceship that would never fly again.

WHERE AM I? thought Laika.

She put her tail between her legs and whimpered.

LUCY? she thought.

Then she heard something.

"Woof! Woof! Woof!"

Laika looked about her. She was sure that somebody had woofed. She knew a woof when she heard one, and she was more or less sure that the dog who had woofed was not her. She was pretty certain that when her ears had heard the sounds "Woof! Woof! Woof!" her mouth had been firmly shut. So it *couldn't* have been her.

In which case, it must have been *another* dog.

She padded a little way from *Prototype I.*

"Woof! Woof! Woof!"

Laika stood completely still, her nose trembling. She was *certain* that it was not her doing the woofing. Somebody or other was woofing, and it was not her.

"Woof! Woof! WOOF!"

With the final woof, a door slid open at the far end of the big, gleaming metal room, and through the door bounded a very big, very friendly dog. The dog was shaggy and enthusiastic and a bit bigger than Laika, and its face was very approachable, and it hurtled across the big metal room toward Laika, woofing madly; and Laika, who was so happy to see another dog, started woofing back.

But then she stopped woofing, because she had a

thought. *THERE IS SOMETHING STRANGE ABOUT THIS DOG.*

"Woof! Woof!" barked the dog as it came closer.

Laika hesitated. The dog was more or less like a normal Earth dog, but it was different in a way that Laika could not put her paw on. Of course, there are all kinds of dogs on Earth: big dogs and little dogs, shaggy dogs and dogs without any fur at all, grumpy dogs and friendly dogs, dogs that smell nice and dogs that don't smell so nice. But this dog didn't seem quite like any of them, and it took a few seconds for Laika to realize what it was that made it different.

The dog wagged its tail in a circle.

Most dogs wag their tail from left to right or from right to left; but this dog's tail was going around and around, in a very friendly fashion, a bit like a propeller. It was a strange and puzzling sight. But before Laika had a chance to think it over, the propeller-tailed dog took another couple of bounds, then Laika and the dog were standing nose to nose.

They sniffed each other.

THIS DOG SMELLS VERY ODD, thought Laika.

Friendly, but odd.

Then the big, bone-shaped spaceship started to wobble, just so much that you could call it a wobble, and it started to shake, just so much that you could call it a shake, and if Laika had been able to see it from the outside, which she couldn't because she was inside and you can't really see the outside of something when you are on the inside of it, she would have seen the bone turn around and then zoom off, faster than a meteor or a comet, into the great blackness, into the here, there, and everywhereness of space.

But Laika was much more interested in the propeller-tailed dog, which seemed friendly and twirled its tail, and sniffed at Laika, and woofed just once and started to run to the far end of the gleaming metal room. Laika, who had always liked chasing other friendly dogs, and hadn't done it for a long time now, four or five days at least, chased after, her tail wagging. And she was so filled with the joy of chasing things, which is one of the biggest joys that you can have if you are a dog, that she woofed her own woofs in response, and in this way the two dogs ran to the other end of the gleaming room, away from *Prototype I,* and out through the doors that opened and closed with an almost inaudible *swoosh,* and up a ramp into a big room where it was possible to

look out into space, and see the stars scattered across the heavens, and see where several other dogs were looking very busy indeed. Some of them were doing very doggy things, like eating and chasing each other; but others were behaving in a fashion that was really very undoggy indeed. For example, some of them were pushing buttons with their noses and with their paws, and some of them were looking very closely at computer screens and making the kinds of sounds that dogs sometimes make when they are thinking very hard, or else when they are dreaming. The dogs that were not concentrating hard and staring at computer screens looked around at Laika and woofed in welcome and propellered their tails, which Laika assumed meant that they were pleased to see her. Laika woofed back.

The dog who had come to meet her then hopped into a little harness. It started to press some buttons on a

control panel with its big, hairy paw. Laika had no idea what it was doing, but she felt happy and at home and as if she had friends. So she found a nice, comfortable corner where there was a big, soft cushion. She sat down and sighed.

The cushion smelled a bit funny; everything smelled a bit funny in this strange, new world, but it was at least as comfortable as anything that Laika was used to. She curled up contentedly and snuggled down into the cushion.

Outside the window the stars streaked past.

Lucy

Eight years after her first visit, Lucy returned to the Observatory on the Hill.

It was a beautiful, peaceful night. She could hear the hum of night insects and could see the stars scattered overhead. She climbed the steps, her bag slung over her shoulder, and she looked up to the sky. Then she let out a big sigh. "Well, Lucy," she said to herself. "This is it. A new job!"

Then Lucy knocked on the door.

The door opened, and inside stood the director. He was grinning. "Lucy," he said, putting out his hand. "Come on in. Welcome. Please, call me Jim. You remember this place, of course? We're *so* pleased that you've come to work for us."

The director, or Jim, as Lucy now called him, showed

her to her new office. It was a comfortable, cluttered kind of office, with one of those chairs that spin around and have wheels, so that—if nobody is looking—you can send yourself scooting and spinning across the room. On Lucy's desk there was a computer and a big pile of paper ready for her, and a nice box of chocolates to welcome her. Next to the computer was a bulletin board. Lucy smiled.

"I'll go and make a cup of tea," Jim said. "You probably need some time to settle in."

Lucy sat down on the chair and gave it a 360-degree spin, just to test it out. It was a good chair for spinning. Then she reached into her bag and took out an envelope. Inside the envelope was a photograph. It was a picture of her, her mom and dad, and Laika. They were on the beach, and their hair was blowing in the wind. Lucy's dad had asked a passerby to take the photo. It was the summer before Laika disappeared into the here, there, and everywhereness of space, when *Prototype I* was still at the planning stage. They were on holiday at the beach. They were all happy. Laika was positively jumping with joy. Lucy smiled to see the photograph. It had faded slightly. It looked as if all this had happened a long, long time ago.

Lucy took the photograph, and she pinned it up on the bulletin board. "Well, Laika," she said, as much to herself as anything, "here I am! My first proper job!"

At that moment Jim the director came back with a mug of tea. He handed it to Lucy and sat down opposite her. He glanced at the photo of Lucy, her mom and dad, and Laika, and he said, "What an old photo! Was that your dog?"

"Yes," Lucy said. "Her name was Laika."

Lucy reached out and clasped her hands around the mug of hot tea. The warmth was comforting.

Seeing that Lucy needed more time to settle in, Jim left her alone.

Lucy looked at the photo pinned above the desk. In the photo Laika was leaping into the air, her ears floppy and her tongue lolling out. They must have been playing at throwing sticks, because Laika had that slightly mad *THROW THE STICK* look to her. Lucy was grinning.

She remembered the day that the photo had been taken. They were on their summer holiday—Lucy, her mom and dad, and Laika. It had been a good day and a good holiday. On that holiday Lucy had spent a lot of the time drawing up plans for *Prototype I*. She wrote everything down in a blue notebook, and didn't let anybody see what she was doing, because she didn't want her mom and dad interrupting her when she was trying to think very hard about things.

It's a complicated business designing spaceships. You have to know about all kinds of things. You have to know what to build the spaceship out of, and what to use as fuel, and you have to be able to do lots of math so that you can point the spaceship in the right direction, and you have to be good with computers, and you need to think hard about what kind of chairs to have, because they need to be comfy enough to sit in for a long time, but not so comfy that you fall asleep and your spaceship crashes. And Lucy took all of this very seriously indeed, because she was the kind of person who thought that if you were going to design a spaceship, you might as well make a good job of it.

Sometimes, in the evening after a day on the beach, when her mom saw her scribbling in the notebook, her mom asked her, "Lucy, love, what are you doing?"

"Oh, nothing," Lucy replied.

Or else her dad said, "You look like you are concentrating very hard. What *are* you up to?"

And Lucy rolled her eyes and said, "Dad, I'm thinking."

Then her dad smiled, because he found it annoying to be interrupted when he was thinking as well, and he said, "Sorry," and he tiptoed out of the room.

It was only when she got home from her holiday, when she was sure about her plans, that Lucy announced to her parents she was designing a spaceship, and that now that her designs were complete, she wanted to build it. She announced this over dinner, just as they were beginning to tuck into their dessert, and for a few seconds there was a terrible silence.

"Oh," her mom said at last.

"Hmmm . . . ," said her dad.

"A spaceship?" her mom asked.

"A real one? Full-sized?" her dad added.

Lucy went a little bit red. It is always hard to tell other people about things that really matter to you, because you never know if they will matter as much to the people you are talking to. "A real one," she said. "So I can go exploring the universe with Laika."

"Oh," said her mom.

"Hmmm . . . ," her dad repeated.

They both looked thoughtful. Then her dad got a dreamy look on his face, his eyes glazing over, and her mom stood up and went to the cupboard. Her mom returned with a big toolbox. She opened it up. It was full of wrenches and hammers and soldering irons, and bits of wire and other useful things. "Will any of this help?" her mom asked. "Just let me know what you need, and I'll do my best to give you a hand."

Then her dad shook himself and smiled at her. "This is a very interesting project," he said. "A *very* interesting project. I'm afraid that, unlike your mom, I can't give you any practical help. But it looks to me that you'll need to do a whole lot of thinking as well. So if you ever want to come perambulating with me, we can think about things together."

Lucy smiled at her mom and dad. "Thanks," she said. "I'll let you know."

Laika

Laika had just gotten settled when the dog who had met her turned and woofed at her.

"Whuff," it said. "Wuff, fwhuff, awuff."

If Laika had been able to understand every single word that the space dog was saying, she would have known that it was telling her, "Friend, we are about to enter a wormhole." But because she couldn't understand very much, being a not very intelligent dog, she just understood the first bit: "Friend."

FRIEND, she thought, and wagged her tail. "Woof," she said enthusiastically. "Woof! Woof!"

"Whuff!" the dog replied, which in space-dog language means "friend."

Then, before Laika could reply, the ship lurched and shuddered and there was a strange, unsettling, high-pitched noise that made Laika shudder.

Then the ship fell into the wormhole.

"A *what*-hole?" you might ask.

And if you asked this, you would not be alone. Because this is precisely the question that Owen asked Lucy one day when they were still at school. They had been walking to school together and talking about wormholes. Lucy had been reading about wormholes in *New Scientist,* and she was trying to tell Owen about them. Owen was looking as if he didn't quite get it.

They arrived at school and went straight into Mr. Kingham's science lesson. They were studying forces or something like that. Lucy found it too easy. Owen found it a little difficult. After the lesson Lucy and Owen were sitting on a bench in the schoolyard, swinging their legs, and talking about this and that and the other.

"I still don't get it," said Owen.

"Don't get what?" Lucy asked.

"Wormholes? In *space*?" he asked Lucy.

"Yes," said Lucy patiently.

"Made by real space worms?"

"Er, no," said Lucy. "Not made by actual *worms.*"

"Oh," said Owen. He looked disappointed. Then he took out his notebook and showed Lucy a picture. "Look," he said. "I drew this in our science class."

It was a picture of a space worm. The space worm was long and bobbly and had big, terrifying eyes and sharp teeth, and it was a very good drawing indeed. The space worm was about to gobble up a planet. The planet had rings like Saturn. Underneath, Owen had written the words "Space Worm."

All of this was of course very interesting, but it didn't have anything to do with wormholes. "Wormholes have nothing to do with worms," Lucy explained patiently. "The worms are a metaphor."

Owen looked puzzled and a little disappointed. "A *what*?" he asked.

"Oh, never mind," said Lucy. "The point is, this is just a way of speaking. It's not about actual *worms*. They're called wormholes because they are sort of holes that you can use to worm your way from one bit of space to another."

Owen had no idea what Lucy was talking about. He was still thinking about space worms, and imagining their sharp teeth, and wondering whether they were big enough to eat planets and moons and things. Nevertheless, Lucy did her best to explain it. And it was actually pretty interesting. Because the thing about space travel is that

even if you go very, very fast—close to the speed of light, which is something like 186,000 miles per second—it will take you more than four years to get to the nearest star. But this is where wormholes come in. Wormholes are like shortcuts in space that can get you from here to there, *but without going through any of the places in between.* This is handy, as Lucy explained, because if you can get from here to there without going through any of the places in between, then you can keep from wasting quite a lot of precious time.

Owen still looked puzzled, so Lucy took a piece of paper out of her bag. "I'll show you," she said. "Imagine that all of space is this sheet of paper."

"OK," said Owen. He sounded a little bit suspicious, as if Lucy were about to pull a trick on him.

Then Lucy drew two dots on the paper, one at each side. She marked the first dot "A" and the second dot "B." "Here's a question. What is the quickest way of getting from A to B?"

Owen frowned.

"Draw it on the paper," said Lucy. She handed Owen a pen.

Very carefully, Owen drew a straight line from A to B.

"Wrong!" shouted Lucy with a big grin on her face.

"What do you mean, 'wrong'?" Owen protested.

Lucy picked up the paper and looped it so that A and B were almost touching. "That's the quickest way."

"That's cheating," said Owen.

"No it's not. That's how it works!" Lucy said. And she had such a serious look in her eye that Owen didn't dare argue. "I know it *looks* a little bit cheaty, but that's what a wormhole is. If you imagine that this paper is all of space, then if you can find a loop in space like this, you can go from A to B, even if they are billions and billions of miles apart, as quickly as you can get to shops. You just pop into the wormhole at one end, and you pop out billions and billions of miles away."

Owen nodded slowly. Then he looked strangely thoughtful and stared off into the distance for a few moments.

"What are you thinking about?" Lucy asked him.

"I'm wondering whether they have *teeth*," Owen said.

"Whether *what* have teeth?" Lucy asked.

"The space worms."

Lucy sighed. Owen was nice, but he was hard to talk to sometimes.

Somewhere, far off in the distance, was a giant, bone-shaped spaceship hanging in the middle of the blackness of space. And if you were looking at the scene, one moment you would see the bone-shaped spaceship, all gleaming and white. And the very next moment you would see it pop out of existence as if it had *entirely disappeared.*

Then you would rub your eyes and think, *How very strange!* And unless you knew about wormholes and things like that, you would tell yourself that you were probably imagining things.

But it would be even stranger if you were at the *other end* of the wormhole. Because one moment you would be looking at a bit of space and there would be *nothing at all there;* and the next moment there would be a giant, gleaming bone floating in the middle of space where, just now, there was nothing. And if you saw this, and of course if you didn't know about wormholes, you would probably think that you were going mad, because *things don't just appear like that.*

But sometimes they do.

Because that is exactly what happened.

Lucy

One evening Lucy was sitting in the observatory. It was late and almost everybody had gone home. There was only the whirr and hum of the machinery and the soft purr of Ptolemy, the observatory cat, who was fast asleep on top of a particularly warm bit of equipment. Ptolemy was a stray. Lucy had found him outside a couple of years before, mewling to be let in, and so they had decided to adopt him. He didn't really do much—mostly he slept— but Lucy liked having him around.

Lucy tidied up the papers on her desk and rubbed her eyes. It was late and she was tired. Ptolemy purred softly in his sleep. Lucy looked at him and felt just a little bit jealous that she, too, wasn't already asleep. Then, just as Lucy was getting ready to go home, she heard a knock at the door. She spun her chair around and shouted, "Come in!"

The door opened and in came Jim, the director. He was out of breath from climbing up the steps, and he had a letter in his hand.

"Hello," said Lucy. "Are you looking for me?"

"Lucy," said Jim, "I'm glad I caught you. A letter arrived this morning. Special delivery. I was so very busy that I completely forgot to give it to you."

"Oh," said Lucy. "Where is it from?"

"Sweden," Jim said.

"Sweden? I don't know anybody in Sweden. . . ." Lucy looked puzzled. She pushed back her chair and got to her feet. Jim handed her the letter.

"What is it?" she asked. "A birthday card? It's not even my birthday for a few weeks, but you never know. . . ."

She looked at the letter. It looked quite official and important. It didn't look much like a birthday card.

"I think you should open it," said Jim. His mustache was quivering a little.

Lucy opened up the letter and started to read.

"Dear Lucy," it said. "We are delighted to inform you that, due to your contributions to astronomy and to the understanding of the here, there, and everywhereness of space, the committee for the Nobel Prize in Physics has decided to present you with an award. . . ."

The letter was friendly but rather formal. Lucy read it through several times. Then she folded it up and put it back in the envelope. Jim was looking at her with eager eyes.

"I think I've won the Nobel Prize," Lucy told him.

Jim beamed. Then he chuckled and did a strange

little dance. Lucy had never seen Jim dance before, and it made her laugh.

Jim ended his dance with a low bow and then grinned at Lucy. "Lucy," he said, "this is the best news I have had in *years.* I'm delighted. Not surprised, of course, but I'm delighted nevertheless. You should go home and celebrate."

Lucy felt like she was in shock. "I think I'll give my mom and dad a ring," she said.

"OK. Well, I'm off," said Jim. "Remember to lock up when you leave. And well done again."

"Thanks," said Lucy.

She watched Jim leave, then she took her phone from her bag and dialed her mom and dad's number. "Hello," her mom said at the other end.

"Hello," said Lucy. "It's Lucy."

"I know," said her mom. "Hello. Are you OK?" Her mom thought that Lucy's voice sounded a little strange, and this made her anxious.

"I'm fine, Mom. I'm just calling you to tell you I won a prize."

"You won a what?" Lucy's mom's hearing wasn't what it used to be.

"A prize," Lucy yelled.

"Oh, a prize," her mom said. "That's nice. What was it? A box of chocolates? A bottle of wine?"

"Er, no," said Lucy. "It's the Nobel Prize."

"The what?" her mom asked.

"The Nobel Prize," Lucy repeated, louder this time.

At the other end of the line there was silence. Then

her mom let out a huge, excited *"Whoooooop!"* Lucy could hear her dad's voice in the background, saying to her mom, "Good gracious! What are you whooping for?"

"She's won the Nobel Prize," her mom yelled.

"The what prize?" Lucy's dad's hearing was not very good anymore either.

"The NO. BEL. PRIZE!" her mom shouted.

For a moment there was silence at the other end of the line. Then Lucy heard her dad's voice in the background. "The NO. BEL. PRIZE?" he asked.

"Yes, dear," her mom said. "The NO. BEL."

There was another pause. Then she heard her dad say, "Gosh! Tell her 'Gosh!'"

"Your dad says, 'Gosh!'" Lucy's mom said.

"Yes, Mom. I heard him. I'm going to Sweden to collect it," Lucy said. "I want you both to come with me."

She heard her mom let out a little sob. "We'd love to," said Lucy's mom. "We'd love to."

Eventually Lucy put down the phone. She felt both happy and sad at the same time, something that people sometimes say is impossible, but something that is much more common than you might think.

Oh, wow, thought Lucy. *Oh, wow! Oh, wow! Oh, wow!* Then she left the observatory and locked the door behind her. Above she could see the stars of the Milky Way. All around her was the hum of night insects. Overhead she saw a shooting star streak past.

Oh, wow, Lucy thought again.

Laika

There is no way of writing down the sound that you hear if you are in a bone-shaped spaceship and you pop out on the other side of a wormhole. You could write it like this—*proop-plung-plung-plop*—but that wouldn't be quite right. Or you could write it like this—*bjoop-bhung-mwung-mwob*—but that wouldn't be right either. You could try writing it in some other language, perhaps in Arabic or Chinese. And you'd still not be able to write it properly because it is one of those sounds that is so very strange, and that comes and goes so very quickly, that it is only a few seconds later that you say to yourself, "That was a most peculiar kind of sound. I wonder how I could write it down." And by this time it is already too late.

And besides, this is a sound that nobody on Earth has ever heard, so there really is no way of checking which way of writing it is correct. Let us just say, then, that the spaceship made the most peculiar noise, one that made Laika go, "Woof! Woof! Woof!" And then the ship popped out of the other side of the wormhole.

Out of the window of the spaceship Laika saw a funny thing. Ahead of the ship was a distant star and what looked like another big ball hanging in space.

BALL! Laika thought, and started to woof very excitedly.

But it wasn't a ball at all. It was a planet that was orbiting around a star called Alpha Centauri A, a star that is, as Lucy knew, roughly twenty-five trillion six hundred and thirteen billion two hundred and sixty-three million two hundred and ninety-six thousand and fifty-five miles away from Earth; and for the dogs piloting the spaceship, the dogs who were busy pressing buttons with their paws, the planet was home.

The bone spaceship started to move toward the planet, and the planet got bigger and bigger and bigger. Laika stopped woofing and gazed out of the window, not knowing what to think.

The spaceship turned on its axis, and it started to come in to land. There was a soft hum. The dogs pressed their buttons with looks of doggy concentration. Even their propeller tails were still. And Laika, who had the funny feeling that something important was happening, but who didn't know what, pressed her nose to the window and stared.

Landing on the planet was a much less scary business than the takeoff had been. The bone spaceship

came to land so very gently that it was almost as if nothing at all had taken place. The space dogs turned off their machines and let out a big, collective "Woof!"

Then the door of the spaceship swung open.

Lucy

The days leading up to the Nobel Prize ceremony were busy. You'd think that getting a prize was the easiest thing in the world, that you just had to turn up and smile a bit and shake people's hands and so on. But things are never that simple. It was hard enough, Lucy thought, winning a Nobel Prize. But it seemed almost as hard organizing everything you had to do to pick it up.

So Lucy had to make all kinds of plans, sign all kinds of documents, make lots of phone calls to Sweden, and generally do a lot of organizing. She also had to get in touch with all the friends who had sent her congratulations cards. Owen sent one that he had made himself—a beautiful drawing of a planet with rings around it. Professor Cassiopeia sent one marked, "To my best-ever student." Even Mr. Kingham sent a letter—a proper, old-

fashioned letter, written by hand. In his letter Mr. Kingham said that he had now retired, and that he had lots of
time on his hands. He said that he had, on a whim, sub-
scribed to *New Scientist*, and that he had read an article
about Lucy, so he thought he'd send her a letter. "You
always were *much* more clever than me," he wrote in his
letter. "Let me tell you a secret: I never really understood
relativity until you explained it in my class. . . ."

Eventually all the organizing was done, and Lucy
packed her bags. She took down the photograph from
above her desk in the observatory—the one that had
been taken by the passerby on her family's summer
holiday—and put it between the pages of a book. Then
she slipped her book into her bag. Finally, she went
home to pick up her mom and dad, and together they all
got on a plane to Stockholm, the capital of Sweden.

On the plane Lucy's mom and dad talked excitedly,
but Lucy was quiet and thoughtful. She was thinking
about the Nobel Prize, which seemed to be really quite
a lot of fuss. The prize was going to be presented by
the king of Sweden. She had never met a king before,
whether of Sweden or of anywhere else, and she wasn't
sure that kings were the kinds of people she wanted to
spend time with. Lucy was sure that the king was a perfectly nice man, but as she looked out of the airplane
window, she found herself thinking that being a king
can't be lots of fun. You have to wear funny outfits, and
sit through long, boring ceremonies, and look all kingly.

So what Lucy was thinking about most was not meeting the king of Sweden, but instead the speech that she

was going to give two days before the award ceremony. All the prizewinners had to give a speech, and Lucy wasn't really used to giving big speeches, so she was both excited and a little worried. *What should I say?* she thought as she looked out of the window at the ground far below.

When they arrived in Sweden, they were met at the airport by some important-looking people who drove them in a big black car to their hotel. The hotel was so *very* posh, and everybody was so *very* polite, that it made Lucy want to pull silly faces. But Lucy reminded herself that it was the Nobel Prize, and that there were kings and people like that involved, and that pulling faces in front of the king might seem strange, or odd, or treasonous. So she decided instead to behave herself.

Lucy, her mom, and her dad had three days in Stockholm before the ceremony. She let her mom and dad go and explore the city—her dad found some parks to perambulate in, and her mom spent most of her time in museums—while she stayed in her hotel, writing her speech. She tried to make it as impressive as possible, filling it with startling thoughts about the here, there, and everywhereness of space. By the time it came to the night of the speech, she had worked so hard that she was not at all sure if it was a good speech or a bad speech. Either way, it was too late. A big black car picked up her, her mom, and her dad and drove them to the hall where she was going to make the speech. There were lots of introductions and lots of people to meet. But then, at last, Lucy stepped out onto the stage and she walked over to the podium. The audience clapped and cheered. Lucy took her place at the podium and cleared her throat.

Laika

The door of the spaceship swung open, and Laika peeped out. She was standing at the top of a slanting gray metal ramp that led down to the ground. There was a sun glinting up in the sky. In fact, there were two suns, which was puzzling. One was really quite big, and the other was much smaller, but both were shining cheerfully. There was grass at the bottom of the ramp, or something like it, but it wasn't the kind of grass that Laika recognized. Even from where she stood on the ramp, she could tell that the grass smelled funny, *almost* like grass on Earth, but *not quite.*

What Laika didn't know, what she couldn't know—because she was only a dog, and this kind of thing would be too difficult even for the most clever dog that had ever lived—was that she was around twenty-five trillion six hundred and thirteen billion two hundred and sixty-three million two hundred and ninety-six thousand and fifty-five miles away from home, on a planet orbiting the star Alpha Centauri A, which was the bigger of the two suns in the sky. The second, smaller sun was Alpha Centauri B. In reality, Alpha Centauri B is only a little bit smaller than Alpha Centauri A, but to Laika it looked much smaller, as it was much farther away.

Laika didn't think, *THERE ARE TWO SUNS*, because even this kind of thought is quite a difficult thought to have if you are a dog. Perhaps if you are a clever dog, you might manage to have a thought that complicated. But Laika was not a clever dog. She was a friendly dog, but not a clever one. So Laika's thoughts were really much, much simpler. As she stood at the top of the ramp, she found herself thinking, *THIS IS STRANGE.* Not frightening-strange—Laika wasn't frightened—but strange nonetheless.

There were trees, too. Tall, bobble-shaped trees that rustled a little in the cool breeze that was blowing from the distant mountains. They had trunks that were very thin and went straight upward as high as a house before breaking out into clusters of branches and leaves.

THIS IS STRANGE, thought Laika again. The trees did not look like the trees at home; and on the breeze there were tree smells that were not like the tree smells of home; and the light, now that she thought about it, was not like the light of home.

Then there was a woofing and a barking from behind her, and the pack of space dogs, obviously happy to be home, came hurtling out of the bone-shaped space-ship and into the grass, and there they turned around and bowed down the way dogs do, putting their chins on the ground between their paws, spinning their tails in big, excited circles, and barking in a friendly *Come on* kind of way, the way Laika would sometimes bark when she wanted to go for a walk with Lucy.

Something about the barking made Laika think of Lucy: it seemed an age since she had last seen her. And it had been an age. In Laika time it had been a whole week: five days of traveling in *Prototype I,* one day of traveling with the space dogs toward the wormhole, not very long at all inside the wormhole, and a day on the other side of the wormhole. And if you are a dog, a week feels like a long time. It feels almost like forever.

THIS IS STRANGE.

Fleeting thoughts of Lucy crowded Laika's head. But then she let out a bark at the dogs who were trying to encourage her to come and join them on the grass, and she galloped down the ramp and rolled around in the grass, and it smelled good, and the dogs rolled around with her, barking at her and wagging their tails and nudging her, there under a strange and distant star, and Laika had a thought that, if it were possible to translate it into human language, would look something like this:

THIS IS PARADISE.

If you are a dog, the things you want out of life are relatively simple. Human beings want all kinds of com-plicated things: they want to be king or queen or prime minister; they want to be famous; they want to own a big car; they want a new computer; they want to know what would happen if you traveled close to the speed of light; and they want to know if it's *really* possible that, one day, a dog could fly off into space in a spaceship built by a girl who was still in school. But dogs want much more simple things: they want friends, and they want food, and they want to play, and they want people to be nice to them, and they want . . . rabbits.

RABBITS! Laika thought.

"Gavagai!" said one of the space dogs in a gruff and doggy voice, a word that might, if we'd been able to translate it, mean "Rabbits!"

And Laika looked through the grass to see—only a few feet away, just on the other side of a small hillock—a rabbit, crouching and nibbling. It was, in almost every respect, exactly like a rabbit: it had a twitching rabbity nose; it had rabbity feet, the front ones neat and tidy, the back ones powerful and good for jumping; it had a rabbity tail, and a very fluffy one at that; but it also had three rabbity ears.

EARS, Laika thought.

She didn't think, *THREE EARS,* because she couldn't quite count. But there was something about the ears that wasn't as she expected it should be. The rabbit had one ear to either side of its head, and one in the middle that stood bolt upright. It was definitely a rabbit. A rabbit with three ears, no doubt, but in all other respects a rabbit. And Laika, being a dog, liked nothing more than chasing rabbits. She was not fussy. She had chased a lot of two-eared rabbits in her time. Once she had chased a one-eared rabbit. This was her first three-eared rabbit, but it was clearly a rabbit. It even smelled like a rabbit, *almost.*

The space dogs turned to watch Laika, who was watching the rabbit. Then the rabbit held up its head, waggled it from side to side, sniffed the air, and started to hop away.

RABBIT! Laika thought, and she bounded after it.

The rabbit was fast. It ran through the grass under the alien sun, faster than any Earth rabbit, and Laika gave chase. It was then that she noticed that the other dogs had all scattered, because on this particular planet, rabbits were everywhere. And if you are a dog, finding yourself surrounded by rabbits is one of the best things that could ever happen to you. If you are a dog, there is nothing, absolutely nothing, nothing on the whole Earth, nothing in the whole universe, more fun than a planet full of dogs to make friends with and rabbits to chase.

"WOOF! WOOF!" barked Laika.

"Gavagai! Gavagai!" barked the space dogs.

Hop! Hop! went the rabbits. They seemed to be enjoying the game as well.

And this is what they did all day, as the sun set over that strange and distant world, with its bobble trees and odd-smelling grass. Not once did any of the dogs manage to catch a rabbit because the rabbits were fast and cunning, but the chase was the most important thing. They chased and chased as the sun set, and then when it started to get dark, the rabbits got bored of the game and hopped back into their burrows to curl up for the

night, happy and content, and Laika and the space dogs all lay down in the grass, exhausted and panting, as two strange moons came up over the planet. They lay there for a while, snuggled together, then they fell asleep underneath the winking stars.

Lucy

Lucy paused and looked out at the audience, waiting for the clapping to subside. Because all the lights were on the stage, shining into her eyes, it took a moment for her eyes to adjust. Then she saw her mom and dad in the front row, and she smiled at them.

Wow, Lucy thought. *Here I am in Stockholm, giving a speech for winning the Nobel Prize. Wow!*

Then Lucy looked down at the speech she had written. She had been told that this was the biggest and most important speech of her life, but when her eyes scanned over the words, the speech didn't seem quite right.

The clapping came to an end, and Lucy cleared her throat. She had no idea what she was going to say. She looked at the people in the front two rows of seats. They all seemed very well-dressed and important. Lucy thought they looked hard to impress. They didn't look like the kind of people who liked lying on the grass and looking up at the stars. They looked like the kind of people who would say, "You expect me to lie on the grass and look at the stars? Are you *mad*? Do you know how much this dress cost?" But then she reminded herself that this was, after all, a Nobel Prize speech. They probably didn't always dress up like that. And she, too, wasn't dressed for lying on her back and looking up at the stars. So she told herself not to be too intimidated, and reminded herself that, given a chance, *everyone* liked looking up at the stars and wondering.

The audience members were leaning forward in their chairs, expectant, as if Lucy were about to explain all the secrets of the here, there, and everywhereness of space.

What shall I say? Lucy thought. She caught her mom's and dad's eyes, smiling up at her from the front row. Then she thought of Laika, and at that moment Lucy made a decision.

She carefully folded up the paper on which she had written her big, impressive speech, and she put the paper in her pocket. She smiled at the audience. "Good evening," she said. "I am sure you are all here because you want to hear me say some big, clever things about space and time and the universe. And I'll say a bit about some of these things, even if I cannot guarantee that what I say is particularly big or clever."

At this point there was a murmur of anxiety in the audience, because they had hoped very much to hear Lucy say big, clever things.

Lucy went on. "Before coming here, I wrote out a very important-sounding speech for you. But I've changed my mind. I don't want to read my important speech. Instead I want to tell you a story."

Here Lucy paused. A woman all decked out in pearls, who was sitting in the second row, frowned.

"It is a story about a brave and rather untidy dog," Lucy said. "And I want to tell you this story because, had it not been for this brave and rather untidy dog, I do not think I would be standing here today. . . ."

The woman in the second row looked a bit annoyed, as if she hadn't come to hear a talk about a *dog.* She pursed her lips in displeasure. Lucy's glance flickered along the line. She saw her mom and dad again, and grinned at them. Then she looked a little more fiercely at the audience, the way people look when they know that what they are saying is important, even if nobody else realizes it yet. "Her name was Laika," she said.

Then Lucy started to talk. She talked about one day when Laika had broken into the cupboard and eaten all the dog biscuits. She talked about the walks that they used to go on. She talked about *Prototype I.* She talked about the terrible, terrible night when Laika blasted off into space. She talked about how she had looked and looked and looked for Laika, but her dog had never returned. Then she took out the photograph of her, her mom and dad, and Laika, and held it up for the audience to see. Luckily, her speech was being projected on big TV screens, so the cameras homed in on the photograph, and everybody saw the picture—how long ago it seemed, like something from ancient times!—of Lucy

and her mom and dad, the wind blowing all of their hair, and Laika in midair. She talked about Mr. Kingham and Owen and relativity and Einstein, and how Einstein liked pulling faces. She even pulled some faces of her own (which made most of the people in the audience laugh, even though it made the woman with the pearls frown as if she had been personally insulted). She talked and talked about the here, there, and everywhereness of space, with lots of jokes and stories. And as she talked, the people in the audience felt themselves fill with wonder and excitement, and leaned even farther forward so that they wouldn't miss a single word.

Then Lucy came to the end and realized that she had no more to say. "That is all I have to tell you," she said. "And so I want to thank you all for your patience in listening to my talk. I want to thank my mom and dad, who are so happy to see me standing here today. I want to thank my old teachers, all my friends at the observatory, all of you in the audience—and of course the Nobel Committee for Physics, who have awarded me this honor."

She hesitated again, and her voice became very small and quiet. She looked up to the roof of the auditorium, as if she could see straight through it to the skies beyond, and she said, "But most of all, I want to thank you, my lovely Laika. This prize is dedicated to you." Then she smiled softly and lowered her head.

There was silence for a moment. A loud sob came from the second row. The woman in pearls pulled out a huge handkerchief, dabbed her eyes, and blew her nose.

She rose to her feet. "Bravo!" she cried in a deep, rumbling voice. "Bravo!"

Then somebody else at the back stood up and shouted, "Laika! Bravo for Laika!" And all of a sudden, everybody in the auditorium was on their feet and cheering, and shouting, and sobbing and hugging each other and calling out Laika's name, and saying, "Bravo!" And Lucy, standing in front of them all, smiled through her tears and held up the photo of Laika, and the photo was projected on the screen behind her.

Oh, Laika! she thought. *My brave, beautiful Laika!*

Once the evening was over, when they were back in the hotel, Lucy sat quietly with her mom and dad, sharing a cup of cocoa before bed. It had been fun being with all the important, glamorous people at the award ceremony, but they were glad that it was over. "We're proud of you, Lucy," her dad said. "We're really proud."

Her mom smiled and reached out to hold her hand. "We're proud of you both," she said. "Both you and Laika."

"Me too, Mom," said Lucy. "Me too."

They finished their cocoa and said good night. Then Lucy went to her room and she closed the door. She put on her moon-and-stars pajamas. Then she stood by the big window of her hotel room and looked out over the city. The night was clear, and she could see the moon hanging over the rooftops. She gazed at the sky for a long time.

Laika

There is no way Lucy could have known, no way she would *ever* know, that while she was looking up at the sky from her hotel in Stockholm, Laika was spending her days with the space dogs, chasing three-eared rabbits, having fun on a distant planet with its bobble trees, and then curling up to snooze contentedly at night in the grass. There are a lot of things in the world that there is no way of knowing, however good your telescope or however hard you look and think about them.

Sometimes, when Lucy looked at the sky, she thought that it was as if she didn't know very much at all.

As for Laika, this was the best holiday she had ever had. Not only were there bobble trees and funny-smelling grass and dogs to play with and rabbits to chase, but there were rivers to leap into, and places to roll around and have fun, and sandy bits of ground where you could spend hours digging holes, and bushes that you could hide under and then leap out from to surprise your friends, and it was as close to paradise as it could be—all except for one thing. And it was this one thing that made her feel just a little bit sad.

Lucy.

The days went past, and every day Laika missed Lucy just a little bit more.

LUCY, Laika thought as she chased the space rabbits.

LUCY, she thought as she played with the space dogs.

LUCY, she thought as she lay down to sleep in the odd-smelling grass.

LUCY, she thought as she looked up at the bobble-shaped trees.

LUCY, she thought as she muttered and twitched and whimpered in her dreams.

LUCY, she thought as she dug holes in the sand, as she swam in the river, as she played with the space dogs, as she chomped on tasty space dog biscuits.

LUCY.

LUCY.

LUCY . . .

Lucy

The final few days in Sweden were busy. Lucy went to the award ceremony two days after her speech and met the king of Sweden. She thought he seemed nice but a little tired. But then, being a king must be hard work, she thought. "I watched the recording of your speech," the king said when he met her. "You must have loved Laika very much." Lucy wasn't sure, but she thought the king looked a little teary.

Lucy thought that it was nice of the king to mention Laika. "Yes," she said. "I do."

Lucy's mom and dad had fun exploring the city. Lucy had lots of official things to do and had to appear on television and radio and in the newspapers. Everybody was very kind and friendly. But by the last night she had had enough of the limelight and was ready to go back to the observatory.

They flew home at night. Lucy looked out of the plane window, high above the clouds. The frosty stars winked at her. She winked back just once. Then she smiled to herself. And somewhere a long way off—to be precise, twenty-five trillion six hundred and thirteen billion two hundred and sixty-three million two hundred and ninety-six thousand and fifty-five miles away, more or less, which is more miles than you could ever count—Laika looked up at the sky and thought of Lucy.

So there they were, twenty-five trillion six hundred and thirteen billion two hundred and sixty-three million two hundred and ninety-six thousand and fifty-five miles apart, both of them looking at the sky and wondering.

Then Lucy sighed and closed her eyes. The plane engine throbbed and hummed in the background. Lucy slipped into sleep. And as she slept, she had such vivid dreams that she could even hear Laika's voice, as clear as it was when she had last heard it.

Woof! Woof! WOOF!

She woke up just as they were coming in to land.

Laika

Woof! *Woof! WOOF!*

Laika woke up and barked at the two suns rising in the sky. *LUCY!* she thought.

A space rabbit popped up over the hill, waving its three ears.

LUCY! she thought.

Two of her new friends came and nuzzled with her and barked in a way that meant "Let's play!"

LUCY! she thought.

And then Laika felt like she didn't want to play anymore. She lay down on the grass and put her snout on the ground, and her ears flopped to either side, and she started to whimper.

LUCY! she thought.

LUCY!

LUCY!

The space dogs, seeing that Laika seemed out of sorts, clustered around to see what was wrong, their propeller tails spinning in consternation.

"Aruff! Gnuffl! Rhaaoww! Grunff!" said one dog.

"Wowff! Aruff! Aruff!" said another.

"Hnuff! Rhaoow! Rhaaow!" said a third.

And if anybody had been around to translate, anybody who had known the language of the space dogs, they might have understood the conversation like this:

"This poor dog is missing home."

"Poor thing! She's come so far!"

"Let's help her get back."

So the dogs nuzzled Laika's ears to comfort her, and made friendly woofing noises, and led her back to the bone-shaped spaceship and up the ramp. Laika didn't really know what was going on, but she knew that they were friendly and she trusted them. So she padded after them, back up the ramp, where she took a last look at the planet with its two suns and three-eared rabbits and the funny-smelling grass. Then she went to lie down in the comfy basket. The space dogs pulled up the ramp and there was a gentle humming sound.

The bone-shaped spaceship took off, very gently, exactly the way that it had landed, and very soon the planet was just like a ball hanging in space. Then they popped through a wormhole with a noise that really can't be described, and popped out the other side. When the ship was floating in the middle of space, just like a gleaming white bone, the space dogs led Laika back to

the huge room where she had first arrived in the space-ship. There, where once *Prototype I* had been, was a large, ball-shaped space pod. It was very smart-looking, with lots of flashing lights on the outside and with an open door through which Laika could see comfortable cushions and places to sleep. In fact, it had everything that a dog might need for a journey.

The space dogs said goodbye to Laika in the way that dogs do, nuzzling and sniffing, and Laika went up the steps into the space pod. The door closed behind her, very gently. The last thing she saw of the space dogs was the blur of their tails, spinning around and around to wish her good luck.

After a few moments the space pod began to hum. It was much quieter than *Prototype I*. Then a hatch opened in the big, bone-shaped spaceship, and the little space pod blasted out of the hatch and into the blackness beyond.

It began to get faster . . . and faster . . . and faster. . . .

Vrrrooooommmmm! said the spacecraft, although the noise it made was much more quiet and polite than the noise made by *Prototype I.*

Laika felt her body becoming heavier, just like it had before. "Owwwwwowow!" she said, but this time it was more out of excitement than out of fear, because Laika had already traveled through space once before, and when you do things for a second time, they are never as frightening.

The spacecraft hurtled through the blackness. In Laika's head there was one single thought.

LUCY!

Lucy

When she was sixty-five years old, Lucy left the Observatory on the Hill, and she went back to the house in which she was born. She would miss being in the observatory, but she was tired and wanted some time to herself. Her hair was now white, and when she looked in the mirror, she thought that she looked old, and she didn't really recognize herself. But then she would pull a funny face and the person in the mirror would pull a funny face back, and she would think, *Phew, it's still me!*

When Lucy moved back, she put all kinds of photographs on her walls. There were photographs of the observatory, of her giving the Nobel Prize speech, of her meeting the king of Sweden, of her mom and dad—who were no longer around, but whom she thought of a lot. Everything seemed like it was a long, long time ago. And right in the center, just above the fireplace, there was the picture of that summer holiday, when she was on the beach with her mom, her dad, and her brave little dog, Laika. The photograph was now really old and faded. But it was nice to sit drinking tea and eating biscuits, and look at Laika leaping into the air, and think about how happy they all had been.

Lucy adjusted to her new life quickly. She gardened, she watched TV, she read books, and she spent time with old friends. She sometimes had tea and crumpets with Owen, who had spent most of his life painting pictures and had been quite successful.

As well as keeping up with old friends, Lucy made new friends. In the rest of the time, she grew vegetables (she was particularly proud of her green beans) and she walked in the park and thought about things just as her dad had once walked in the park and thought about things. And life was good.

Lucy was still an agreeable kind of person, a person who talked with enthusiasm about stars and planets and galaxies and nebulae. But she slept lightly during the night, as older people sometimes do, waking up often; and when this happened, she went and looked out of the window at the night sky, standing in her pajamas decorated with stars and moons, and thought about her past. And sometimes she would put on her dressing gown and go outside and set up her telescope, and look into the here, there, and everywhereness of space. And she would remember Laika.

Occasionally, on those nights when she sat in the garden in her pajamas and looked at the stars while thinking about Laika, she thought, If only! If only I had locked the door of *Prototype I*! If only I had called Laika in for dinner when I went in for dinner! If only I'd been a normal little girl interested in normal little-girl things, and not in building space rockets! If only Laika had been a bit less silly and inquisitive! If only things had been different! But then she just said to herself, "Lucy, you are just being a silly old lady. There is no way of changing the past."

The years passed quietly. Lucy's life was not really very exciting anymore. But she enjoyed the routine, and liked planting her bean sprouts in spring and seeing them grow and flower and produce long green beans in late summer and early autumn.

Then one evening, several years after her return home, when Lucy was sitting in the garden in her pajamas, a head popped over the fence.

"Hello," said the head.

Lucy was startled. She took her eye from the telescope. "Hello!" she said.

The head grinned. "What are you doing?"

"I'm looking at the sky," Lucy said. "What are *you* doing?"

"I'm looking at you," said the head. Then there was a scuffling as the owner of the head clambered up to sit on the fence and get a better look. "I'm Astrid," said the owner of the head.

"Astrid?" Lucy said. "That's a good name. It means 'star.'"

"Does it?" asked Astrid. "I didn't know that."

Lucy looked at Astrid. She was about the same age that Lucy had been when Laika disappeared into space.

"We've just moved in next door," said Astrid.

Lucy smiled. "Welcome to the neighborhood," she said.

"Can I look through your telescope?" Astrid asked.

"I suppose so," said Lucy. "If you are careful."

"Brilliant!" said Astrid. Then she hopped over the fence and went over to where Lucy was sitting. "Nice pajamas," she said.

"Thanks," said Lucy. She showed Astrid how to look through the telescope. They looked at Venus and Mars and the moon. Astrid asked all kinds of questions. They were there for a long time, until Astrid's parents came and leaned on the fence and waved at her to come to bed.

Laika

"Errerrrrrng . . . errerrrrrng . . . errerrrrrng . . ."

Vrrroooooommmm!

"Owwwwwowow! Woof! Woof!"

The little space pod tumbled through space. As it did so, all those strange things that happen when you go very, very fast through space happened again, so that time went a bit bendy and funny, but in a way that—if you could do the sums like Lucy could do the sums— made perfect sense.

Laika didn't know anything about sums. She just lay on the comfy cushions in the spacecraft, and woofed occasionally, and pressed her nose to the glass of the window to look out at the sky, and thought of Lucy, and when the bell rang inside the spacecraft and food appeared in the bowl, almost by magic, she ate the food, and in this way she traveled across the vast black expanses of space, toward home.

The journey back in the space dogs' space pod was a little different from the journey she had taken in *Prototype I*. The vrooming was quieter. It was more a background kind of vroom, more than a hum, just loud enough so that you could call it a vroom. And for some reason, on the way home she was not floating all over the place, which made things much nicer.

The space pod hurtled on. When Laika felt tired, she closed her eyes and slept. When she felt hungry, she ate. Most of the time she just dozed, neither completely asleep nor completely awake. When she slept, she dreamed of Lucy.

Lucy

Over the days that followed, while Lucy sat looking at the sky through her telescope in the evenings, Astrid came over more often. When the sun set, and the evening star appeared (which was in fact the same as the morning star, although it appeared at a different time of day), and when Astrid had finished her dinner, she said goodbye to her mom and dad, headed out into the garden, and hopped over the fence. Then she gave Lucy a hand setting up the telescope, and they drank hot chocolate together, and they looked at the stars and planets, and they talked.

Lucy was pleased to have Astrid's company; and Astrid was full of questions. She asked questions like, "How can the morning star be the same as the evening star?" and "Why does Saturn have rings?" and "What's a nebula?" and "How many planets are there in the universe?" and "How big is space?"

Lucy enjoyed answering Astrid's questions and pointing out things through the telescope. But the thing about questions is that every time you answer one, another two or three pop up in its place, so there was really no shortage of questions. Astrid seemed to be bursting with them. "What's the speed of light?" "Why can't anything go faster than light?" "What's the difference between an asteroid, a comet, and a meteoroid?"

Every evening, when it got late, Astrid's mom and dad came outside and leaned on the fence, and waved at Lucy and said, "Come on, Astrid, it's time for bed." And Lucy waved back and said, "Oh, is that the time?" and Astrid clambered back over the fence and left Lucy sitting in the garden, staring up at the stars.

Then one evening Astrid stopped in the middle of her questions and said, "Lucy, I've got one really big, really important question I want to ask you."

"What's that?" Lucy asked, taking a sip of hot chocolate.

Astrid looked thoughtful. "*Why* do you spend so much time looking at the sky?"

"Well," Lucy said, "because it's interesting."

"And why else?"

"I like stars and planets," Lucy said.

"But is that the *only* reason?" Astrid asked.

Lucy thought for a moment. Astrid was clever. She was *insightful*. Lucy put her mug of hot chocolate down on the grass. She didn't talk much about Laika these days. She preferred to keep things to herself. But she thought she might as well tell Astrid everything. "Well," she said, "there are lots of reasons. But perhaps the real reason is that I do it for Laika."

Astrid saw something change in Lucy's face. "Who is Laika?" she asked.

Lucy sighed. "It's a long story," she said.

Astrid shrugged. "I've got lots of time," she said.

So Lucy told her about how she had built *Prototype I*, and about Laika, and about that fateful evening in the garden, and it felt good to be telling Astrid all of this. Then, when she had finished, Astrid grinned at her. "Wow!" she said. "She must be some dog! Do you think she's ever going to come back?"

Lucy gave a sad smile. "It was so long ago, Astrid," she said. "Laika is long gone."

And Astrid thought that she saw tears in the corners of Lucy's eyes, so she changed the subject and thought of a really, really difficult question to ask. "You know empty space?" she said.

"Yes," said Lucy, smiling and wiping her eyes.

"How empty is it *really*?"

"Well," laughed Lucy, "that's a really big question. . . ."

She was still explaining the answer when Astrid's mom and dad came to the fence and called her in for the night.

Laika

The space pod started to make strange noises.

Ker-chunk! it said. *Ker-chunk, ker-chink!*

The space pod was slowing down.

"Woof! Woof!" said Laika. . . .

Vrrroooooommmmm! Ker-chunk! Ker-chink! the space pod replied.

Laika looked out of the window, pressing her nose to the glass. Then she saw something familiar. It was blue and green and perfectly round.

BALL, she thought.

BALL!

And she thought of Lucy. Where was Lucy to throw and catch? She barked, to see if Lucy answered, to see if she would reappear to pick up the blue-and-green ball and toss it through the air.

But Lucy did not appear.

BALL! Laika thought again.

And she started to bark. "Woof! Woof! Woof!"

In the window the ball became bigger and bigger.

"Woof! Woof!" said Laika. "Woof! Woof! Woof!"

Lucy

It was one of those beautiful September evenings, when things are just a little bit frosty and the stars seem exceptionally clear. Lucy and Astrid were sitting and looking through the telescope. Because it was getting cold and would soon be winter, they were both wrapped in blankets, and when they breathed out, their breath hung on the air, a fine mist.

The grass beneath their feet was slightly damp. The stars were twinkling in a friendly way, and the moon was just a sliver. Over their heads, space—deep, dark, black, mysterious space—went on and on, as it always does.

They were looking at Mars, which was particularly bright that evening. Lucy was explaining about the canals on Mars, which were not real canals, even though people once thought they were. But then Lucy realized that she felt a little chilly, and she glanced at her watch and thought to herself that she would really rather be in bed, tucked up and warm.

Just as Lucy was about to say, "It's getting cold. We should call it a night," Astrid, who had her eye to the telescope, let out an odd little cry.

"Lucy," she said, "there's something strange up there."

Lucy looked through the telescope. Astrid was right. Somewhere in the blackness of space there glimmered something strange, like a small star that really shouldn't have been there. Or a planet. Something shining brightly in a place where there should have been only darkness.

Lucy shook her head a little because she thought she was imagining things. But she wasn't imagining things. The star or planet or whatever it was did not disappear.

"Perhaps it's a satellite," she said to Astrid. "Let me take a look."

The star or whatever it was looked like a bright, shining dot. Lucy hunched over the telescope for a few seconds, then turned to Astrid. "I don't know what it is," she said. "I really don't have the foggiest idea. Take another look."

Astrid looked through the eyepiece again. "Me neither," she said.

What Astrid had seen was puzzling. It didn't seem like a planet or a star or a satellite. There was something funny about it. Something very funny indeed.

Then at exactly the same time, both Astrid and Lucy

realized the star was getting bigger. Very slowly, almost so slowly that you didn't notice, it was getting bigger.

Lucy frowned. She could smell the smells of the night: soil and nocturnal flowers and secrets.

"It's getting bigger," said Astrid. She looked up because she didn't need the telescope anymore. It was definitely getting bigger. And fast, too. Soon it was almost as large as the moon.

"Oh, yikes," cried Lucy, spilling her cocoa. "It's coming straight for us."

At that exact moment there was a kind of rushing sound. Astrid staggered to her feet. "What is it?" she gasped. "What is it?"

"I don't know," Lucy whispered in awe.

And if somebody who has spent a lifetime looking at the skies says that she doesn't know, then it must be something very unusual indeed.

Lucy didn't know what to do. She could have said, "Let's go inside," but the thing was coming toward them so fast, and it was so hard to tell where it was going to land, that there seemed no point in going in. Perhaps it would land on the house; then they would be squashed inside. Perhaps it would land on Astrid's house, which would be unfortunate for Astrid's parents. Perhaps it would land in the street and make a big hole. Perhaps it would land in the garden. Or perhaps it would change course at the last moment and go scooting off in another direction entirely, back up into the sky, or sideways.

Astrid and Lucy gazed up at this thing in awe and terror. There was a huge rush of wind. The trees bent over as if they were about to break, and there was a terrible *ROOOAAAARRRR!*

The thing came blazing down from the sky—it was clear now that it was some kind of ball-shaped thing, the size of a garden shed, but perfectly spherical. And then, without any warning, it slowed down and landed with a loud *THUNK!* only a few yards away from where Lucy and Astrid were standing, in the middle of the vegetable patch, squashing a particularly fine bean plant that Lucy had been looking after all summer and that was, until just a moment ago, hanging with hundreds upon hundreds of enticing green beans.

Thunk! Kerplunk! Hiss!

The thing, whatever it was, let out a big jet of steam. There was another clunk, and a big lump of metal fell off one side, squishing a particularly fine zucchini plant.

Astrid was shaking. "Are we still alive?" she asked.

"I think so," said Lucy.

"Astriiiiiid!" It was Astrid's parents, running into their garden, looks of panic on their faces. "What's going on?"

"It's all right, Mom," called Astrid. "It's just a spaceship." Astrid, it turned out, was the kind of girl who didn't lose her head in an emergency. "I'm going to have a look."

Lucy reached out a hand. "Careful, Astrid!" she said. Astrid's dad was clambering over the fence to try and stop her. But Astrid was already out of reach, heading toward the steaming sphere. The thing was made of some kind of metal, but with various lumps and bumps and flashing lights. And on the part facing them was a door.

There was a quiet *shooshing* sound. The door slid open.

Then Lucy heard a voice that she had not heard for a very, very long time.

"Woof! Woof!" went the voice. "Woof! Woof! Woof!"

Astrid stopped. She leaned forward in astonishment with her mouth open. "A dog?" she whispered.

"Laika?" asked Lucy. And although her voice was very different from that of a ten-year-old girl, it was still recognizably Lucy's voice.

"Woof!" went a voice from inside the strange metal ball, a voice that was inescapably familiar.

"Laika!" cried Lucy. Then she left her telescope and ran past Astrid toward the spacecraft. She put her head through the doorway. Inside she could see Laika, who was in a terrible tangle, with various bits and pieces of spaceship caught up around her tail and around her legs.

"Laika!" Lucy said. And she put her arms around the dog and untangled her, then lifted her gently out of the spaceship. "It's been so long!"

Astrid, her mom, and her dad looked on with utter amazement.

But Laika, being a not very clever dog, was not particularly amazed; she was just extraordinarily pleased to see Lucy. She sniffed at her excitedly, licked her face, wriggled in her arms, and made all kinds of happy, squirmy dog noises. Lucy put Laika down on the grass. Laika was heavy, and Lucy was not as strong as she used to be. And then, there in the garden by the space dogs' little space pod, she put her arms around her dog, and then Astrid and her parents watched as Lucy, who had not seen Laika for a whole sixty years, and Laika, who had not seen Lucy for a whole four weeks, stood underneath the sickle moon and the friendly stars and the here, there, and everywhereness of space, and the two of them hugged, and they hugged and they hugged.

"Astrid," said Lucy at last, "come and meet Laika." So Astrid came over, and the two of them fussed over the big, untidy dog, who seemed so very pleased to be home.

Lucy and **Laika**

It was two in the morning when Lucy eventually got to bed. Astrid's mom and dad were a bit overexcited to see a space pod land in the neighbor's garden, and they had to meet Laika and say hello, and reassure themselves that everything was all right and that nothing else terrible or alarming was going to happen that night. They were a bit confused by everything because they didn't see how a dog who had disappeared sixty years ago could suddenly reappear. But Astrid rolled her eyes and said, "Dad, Mom . . . it's just relativity. I'll explain everything to you."

Astrid's mom smiled a tired smile. "Not now, young lady," she said. "It's quite late enough. You need to go to bed. You can tell us tomorrow."

Lucy smiled at them. "Well," she said, patting Laika

on the head, "I suppose we should be getting to bed as well."

They said good night. Astrid, her mom, and her dad went back next door. And Lucy and Laika went inside.

Once she got over her excitement at being home, Laika curled up on the sofa and went to sleep. Lucy sat for a long time, watching Laika sleep. She wondered where her dog had been for so long, but there was no way of telling. So she just sat and watched as Laika snoozed. It should have felt strange, after these sixty years, to have her dog back. But in actual fact it just felt right.

Laika was dog tired after her long journey. She only woke up after lunch the following day, which gave Lucy some time to go out and buy a leash and some dog biscuits and all the other things you need to look after a dog. In the pet shop she also found a lovely blue-and-green ball that she thought Laika would like.

As Lucy ate lunch, Laika ate breakfast. And then, because it was a beautiful afternoon, they decided to go for a long walk. Lucy left the house, knocked on Astrid's door, and invited them along as well. When everybody was organized, the five of them—Lucy, Laika, Astrid, and Astrid's mom and dad—walked out of town and into the countryside. When they let Laika off the leash, she hurtled around and around in circles, leaping into the air. Astrid threw the ball, and Laika fetched.

It was such a beautiful afternoon that everyone wanted to keep walking forever. They climbed stiles and followed footpaths, and at last they came to a small hill that looked over the fields and the hedgerows. Together they climbed the hill. "Phew!" Lucy said as she reached the top. "That was quite a climb. Let's have a rest."

Astrid's mom opened her backpack and took out some snacks that she had brought along. They munched in happy silence. Then, looking at the sun sinking over the horizon, Astrid's mom said, "We should be heading back."

"Of course," said Lucy. "But I think Laika and I will stay a bit longer. We've got some catching up to do."

"You will be all right getting back on your own?"

Lucy grinned. "I've got Laika to look after me."

"OK," said Astrid's mom. "Well, good luck."

They all said goodbye, and Lucy watched Astrid, her mom, and her dad as they walked away down the hill.

Lucy and Laika sat side by side. Lucy leaned into Laika and felt the warmth of her body. Laika seemed calm and happy. The sky grew dark, and above them stars began to appear.

Lucy thought about how strange it all was, how strange and big and confusing and wonderful. She thought about the way that time goes all stretchy and bendy when you go very fast. She thought about how Laika had left her, all that time ago, and how she had now returned sixty years later. She thought about her mom and dad and how she missed them. She thought about her Nobel Prize, which didn't really matter that much, or not as much as other people believed. She thought about Astrid and her mom and dad. And she thought about space, its here, there, and everywhereness. *How good life is!* she thought.

And Laika leaned in toward Lucy. She thought, briefly, about the space dogs, about three-eared rabbits, about the adventures she had lived through but only barely understood. Then she thought . . .

LUCY, LUCY, LUCY.

"Oh, Laika! Laika! Laika!" said Lucy, giving the dog a squeeze. She had tears in her eyes, but they were tears of happiness.

And so there they sat for a long time: on top of the hill, an old lady and a well-traveled dog, sharing an autumn night, while up above their heads the Milky Way appeared, a river of distant suns so vast and endless that none of us—whether person or dog—could ever count their number.

Author's Note

I do not know if it is really possible to build a spaceship in your back garden and send your dog to the stars, although for your dog's sake, I suggest that you do not try. Nevertheless, I should say something here about the name Laika, and the story that inspired this book.

A long time ago, in the year 1957, when people were first building rockets to go into space, and when they were wondering if it would be possible to use rockets to send people into space, somebody had the idea of trying it out with a dog first.

The dog who was chosen to be a space pioneer was named Laika, which means "barker." She was a bit smaller and less untidy than the Laika in this story but—according to those who knew her—every bit as friendly. After some training, the real Laika was put into a rocket and blasted off into the skies in a spacecraft called *Sputnik II.* But here the story becomes much sadder because, in real life, Laika never came back.

A few years later, it was not dogs who were going into space, but people; and most of them *did* come back. But I have always felt sorry for that poor little dog Laika, the original rocket dog. After thinking about her for a few years, I eventually decided to write a story about another dog named Laika—a dog who not only went into space but also managed to find her way home.

Acknowledgments

It takes quite a lot of work to send a dog into space, even a fictional one, so I am grateful for many people's help over the years of writing this book. Amongst the readers who gave advice on early versions of the story are India and Liberty Abbott; Grant Denkinson, who advised on the science; and my agent, Marilyn Malin. I am also grateful to Kelly Delaney at Knopf for her enthusiasm for tales of space dogs and time dilation, and for her perceptive editorial advice. Finally, I am beyond grateful to Elee Kirk, with whom I have been privileged to spend so many years gazing at the night sky, and talking about the here, there, and everywhereness of space. Elee died shortly before the book was completed, but her influence on the story is here, there, and everywhere, and is quite impossible to measure.